DISSOLVE

RICH SHAPERO
DISSOLVE
A NOVEL

TooFar
MEDIA

HALF MOON BAY, CALIFORNIA

TooFar Media
500 Stone Pine Road, Box 3169
Half Moon Bay, CA 94019

Library of Congress Cataloging-in-Publication Data is available.

ISBN: 978-1-7335259-5-4

Cover photographs by Cameron Nelson
Cover design by Adde Russell and Michael Baron Shaw
Artwork copyright © 2016 Rich Shapero
Additional graphics: Sky Shapero

Printed and Bound by CPI Group (UK) Ltd, Croydon, CR0 4YY

25 24 23 22   3 4 5

Also by Rich Shapero

Island Fruit Remedy

Balcony of Fog

Rin, Tongue and Dorner

Arms from the Sea

The Hope We Seek

Too Far

Wild Animus

THIRTY YEARS BEFORE

Was it the land of the living or the land of the dead? Or a place of transit between?

A black woman emerged from the darkness, barefoot on a dirt road. She wore a patterned wrap and balanced a metal tub on her head. Before her a giant moon, white and round, had risen above the world. The woman's steps took her through puddles, where frogs the size of toe bones hopped and chirped. The road bent at a spindly tree. She yawned as she made the turn, and moonlight gleamed on her pearly teeth. A large lizard hung from a branch by its tail, and as the woman passed, it followed her with rotating eyes.

Beside the road was a weathered warehouse, patched with planks. It had a shed roof of corrugated zinc, and moonlight was flowing down it. Through an open transom, two men were visible inside. One held a lantern with an amber flame.

Craag raised the lantern and squinted. He was bald and

short, in his sixties. The dancing flame blotched his red English skin. He started through the warehouse, sliding between two stacks of crates.

The man who followed was half Craag's age, tall and clean-shaven, dressed in white cottons. "It took me an hour to get past the roadblock," Wiley said. He had a high, dark hairline with receding indents on either side. His eyes were deep and his jaw strong. "Checkpoints in all the wrong places."

Craag wasn't listening.

A large geode appeared in the lantern light, two feet across, like a broken egg. Its lip gleamed with druse, its insides glittered with angular crystals. They circled a hill of rock, blue and gold. Labradorite. And beside it a hill of white quartz. Piles of amethyst and river agate.

They were headed toward the rear of the warehouse, winding through chest-high sections of petrified log. A chicken had settled on one. To the left, open crates were balanced atop a scatter of boxes. Wads of packing material were heaped around unloaded pallets. The warehouse was always crowded, with hauls coming and going, but Wiley had never seen it in such disarray.

Boxes of flame carnelian appeared on the right, and beyond them a rank of giant ammonites. "These are something," Wiley stopped. The fossils were three and four feet in diameter, standing on edge. Their spirals were thick, and the rims were knobbed like off-road tires. The opalescent shells glittered and irised as light invaded their translucent coils. Wiley imagined the creatures swimming in primeval waters, dark and fathomless, a place where the face of man had never been seen.

He looked at Craag. "What's this about?"

The floor shook. The ammonites shifted, and the *boom* of bombs echoed at a distance. The shelling had been constant for days. How much longer would it be before the rebels stormed the city?

"Are you alright?" Wiley asked.

Craag nodded absently.

Boom, boom—

Craag pointed toward a corner of the warehouse.

"You've got buyers waiting?" Wiley said. "Things are stacking up." He drew a persimmon from his vest pocket and a knife with a clip point blade from the sheath on his hip.

Wiley cut the persimmon and offered him a slice.

Craag shook his head. "My guts aren't right."

Wiley peered at him. Typhoid, malaria, bubonic plague—

Craag turned away.

"What's going on?" Wiley pressed him.

Craag exhaled. "I find things. That's what I do."

"You're missing her," Wiley said. "I do too."

"I visited her grave yesterday." The words caught in Craag's throat. "She was my life jacket."

Moonlight filtered through a dusty window. Craag closed his eyes. Wiley watched grief teeter him, like a children's game of cans and stones.

"We had a long talk," Craag said. "It was her idea. 'You need to see Wiley.'"

Wiley set the persimmon down, sheathed his knife and put his hand on Craag's shoulder. A year before, the couple had a thriving export business; Craag was a respected gem hunter, mentor to Wiley and other traders on the troubled island.

Craag leaned closer, eyes meeting Wiley's then slipping away. "Something impossible has happened." He rubbed his hand across his forehead.

"I've found a new gemstone," Craag said.

"New?"

"No one's ever seen anything like it." Craag glowered and laughed, then his expression sobered. He clenched his jaw, turned and stepped forward, holding the lantern before him.

Wiley followed, past boulders rising beneath tarps, past rusted shelving crowded with rocks and chisels and augers. Their shadows shifted over the clutter.

They were approaching a dark corner at the back of the warehouse.

"Alright," Craag sighed, as if conferring with someone else.

They passed a rick of picks and shovels, and a barrel full of mud-covered posts. Then Craag halted. He set the lantern on a shelf above a worn packing trunk.

"This is it."

Craag took a key from his pocket and knelt.

He inserted the key in a padlock and turned. *Click.*

He removed the padlock and raised the lid slowly, pursing his lips, eyeing Wiley while the hinge squealed.

"One of my boys comes from a village on the Sahamalaza Peninsula. He brought me a fragment. And another, a few months later. I had him scour the area. He found where they came from."

Craag reached into the trunk and hefted a rock the size of a coconut.

Wiley knelt beside him.

"Look at those things," Craag said.

The rock was lumpy, but where a spike had struck, it had fractured, and the surface was smooth as glass. You could see through it. Inside, the rock looked watery, with tiny islets and tendrils of froth. Suspended in the water was a mass of orbs, each the size of a small pearl. And they too were translucent. Each orb had multiple shells, one inside the other, perfectly concentered.

Craag reached into the trunk and retrieved another fragment. A small one, oblong with waterworn edges, the length of a finger. He pulled at Wiley's shirt pocket and dropped it in. "Don't show that to *anyone*."

Craag rose, cradling the coconut-sized chunk in his arm.

Wiley rose with him.

"The moon wakes them up," Craag said, turning toward a cracked window.

Wiley saw moonlight flash on the glassy fracture. Craag tilted it and the light beamed deeper, reaching orbs hidden within. They were all sided with silver crescents that seemed to jitter and turn as Wiley watched. The orbs were like fireflies in the Buru jungle—each had its own pulse. And the concentered circles were radiating now. The watery rock was like a pool, and each orb was where a drop of rain had fallen.

"Quit your job," Craag said. "Work with me."

Wiley looked up. Craag's expression was grave.

"Raffia is hopeless," Craag said. "You'll never make any money. If there's a coup, your co-op will go up in smoke. With these gems you'll have a future. We'll split everything down the middle."

"I'll do what I can to help. But—"

Craag's eyes grew wider. "When I'm gone—"

"Gems are a mystery to me," Wiley said.

"I'll handle the mining. You're a trader. You can manage the business. And use what you know about textiles to get the rocks out of the port. No one will expect them to be packed with cotton and raffia."

"You're serious."

Craag put the coconut-sized rock back in the trunk. A rill of sweat dribbled past his ear. He raised his fingers, but his wipe missed, and the rill continued to his jaw.

"I can't do this by myself," Craag shook his head. "I can't."

Weariness seemed to unfocus his eyes.

"Men wait their whole lives for a chance like this," Craag said.

Wiley felt the weight of the fragment in his front pocket. He glanced at the trunk. "How much is there?"

"Enough," Craag replied. "The source is on the coast. In a cove."

"You've seen it?"

"I pitched a tent on a dune and dug my heart out. For twelve days. I reached it. I touched its tail, at the surf line. There's a vein of the stuff, under the beach. Millions of them, flowing together." His gaze wandered, following the path of a horde of orbs.

"Where's the cove?"

Craag nodded, as if to say, "Where. That's the question."

"Are we partners?" Craag asked. Then, without waiting for an answer, he pulled a folded paper from his shirt pocket. It was dog-eared and grease-stained.

He regarded Wiley for a moment. Then his chin tucked. Was he laughing?

Craag groaned and swayed, reaching out. His knee buckled—

Wiley circled his waist. Craag was sturdy and muscled, but his body was like a sack of flour now, loose and slumping. It sent them banging against the shelving. The lantern shattered and the flame sputtered out.

Craag convulsed, choking, gasping. Wiley sagged, letting Craag's weight lower them both. The bald head rolled against Wiley's chest, the shaking torso lay across his hips.

In the moonlight, Craag's face looked chalky. A large shard of lantern glass rose through his shin, and a thread of blood trickled down. Wiley's mind raced—a parasite, Craag's heart, the plague— He raised his shoulders, shifting Craag to the side.

"No. Please." Craag turned, grabbing his shirt front. His lips jutted. A groan emerged.

"I'm going for help," Wiley said, finding his feet.

Craag lunged, trying to pin Wiley beneath him. "Stay with me," he said, jerking as if something had stabbed his chest. "Stay—" His body was rigid, he was staring at Wiley. But he seemed not to see him—

"Are you there?" Craag gasped.

· "I'm here." Wiley held on to him.

Craag's eyes closed. The rigor passed from his frame. One hand still gripped Wiley's shirt, but as Wiley watched, Craag's mouth went slack and his breathing slowed. A grim acceptance seemed to invade him. All the things that had troubled Craag moments before appeared to have fled.

Another stab shook him.

"I'm ready to leave," Craag said.

The air around Wiley seemed suddenly dense, heavy and humid. His vision went dark, completely dark, as if it was joining Craag's. The warehouse unmoored, he felt everything tilting—

A sound, hard and sharp, startled him. Like a hundred nuts cracking.

Wiley's eyesight returned. Directly before him, orbs were rising out of the trunk into a slab of moonlight beaming through the transom. The mass glittered and rippled, each orb concentered, like a stream on which rain is falling.

I'm unconscious, he thought. *Dreaming— Where is Craag?*

A weight crushed Wiley's waist.

He looked down. The older man lay across him. His eyes

were closed. His features were taut, struck with the same shock Wiley was feeling. Craag's lips parted. Was he going to speak?

An orb appeared inches from Wiley's nose. A second emerged from his shirt pocket. He caught a scent, sweet, floral, like crushed violets. Wiley struggled for breath, disbelieving, chest clinched.

Craag's body was no longer convulsing. His eyes opened, his rigid features relaxed. He seemed calm. He was watching the orbs.

They were gathering around them.

The orbs began to circle, a glittering vortex, descending to the floor and rising back up.

Wiley's legs felt numb. His face was tingling. The swarm wheeled closer, the spherical jellies packing around— A sigh, like foam. A frothing sound. A ticking like bubbles bursting. Silvered by moonlight and lit from within, the orbs crowded his mouth. Were they drawn to his wind? Or his sight— Like a muffler of silk, they rode over his eyes. Terror, choking and blind— But instead of constricting his breath, the orbs seemed to free it. Instead of blocking his sight, Wiley saw things he might not have otherwise seen.

The orbs were pulsing as one now. The whole galaxy throbbed, its luminous mass swelling and contracting. A sheet of pearls had slid between the two men. More and more crowded into the space.

The orbs were pulling at Craag.

The pressure on Wiley's hips faded, but he was still holding on. A new odor stung his nose. Raw. Metallic. The odor of blood.

Scarlet threads were flowing out of Craag's body. Their numbers grew, like long locks, a bloody shawl flowing back. Craag's bare arm had divots. In the ghostly light, it looked pitted.

Craag was torn from his grasp. The pearly orbs were lifting him. And from his pocked flesh came scarlet orbs. They bobbed and mingled with their pearly brothers. Craag's clothing was gone, and so was his skin. His flesh was luminescent, bubbling with scarlet orbs.

As he rose, Craag looked back.

Nothing had prepared Wiley for what he saw.

Craag's face was a scarlet mask, bright and beaded. But his eyes were lucid, wide with wonder, deep with peace. His expression was blissful. Joy seemed to be welling inside him— the joy of his youth, or the joy he had known before his wife fell ill.

No, Wiley thought. *This is something he's never felt.*

A new joy was announcing itself, a joy that had been a mystery to Craag all his life.

His lips moved. *Wiley*, Craag mouthed, and his gaze matched his voice, blissful, unearthly, free from the ferment at last.

"I'm with them," Craag whispered.

Then his body was lost in the bright pulse.

As Wiley watched, a sheaf of the pearly mass peeled loose, and the whorls with Craag at their center became a scarlet river with the silhouette of a body within. The river circled the warehouse, rushing, its front and sides frothing with silvery orbs while it gained height. Then, all at once, the orbs and the river absorbed the body they carried.

The front of the flow reached the open transom and passed through, into the moonlit night. Its bright tail whipped and vanished.

Wiley's vision blacked. The floor heaved beneath him, a ship's deck in a storm. The air was thick as gravy—

Then, slowly, the choking damp leached away. His breath returned. The rushing faded and the warehouse settled.

Wiley lay still. Then he tried to rise.

Something heavy weighted his hips. Craag was lying on top of him, the shard of lantern glass stuck through his leg. The burden was leaden, unyielding. Wiley shuddered and tasted bile. They were on the warehouse floor. The folded paper, dog-eared and grease-stained, lay two feet away on the planking. The lid of the trunk was open.

Wiley put his fingers to the sweaty neck, hoping, feeling for a heartbeat.

Craag was gone.

1

At the head of the stream, water emerged from solid rock. The flow had scooped the sandstone, giving its pinks and tans the appearance of flesh, and turbulence had dug a pool with a surface as green as a lizard's back. On the pool's downstream side, a giant cottonwood had rooted.

The Old Y had two thick boughs, one arching toward the redrock cliff, the other toward the valley below. Its trunk was gray and tawny and deeply furrowed. Its ranging branches stood leafless in the Utah winter, strands of wild vine tangled among them.

A woman in her thirties, swarthy-skinned and darkly dressed in Indian cottons, halted where the tree's roots knuckled through the red soil. Long black hair circled her face, harnessed by the shawl around her shoulders. The tall man behind her, in a beige coat and white pants, removed his cap.

Wiley passed the woman his walking stick. She leaned it against the Y's trunk, put an arm around his back and, supporting his elbow with the other, helped him over the roots, into the net of shadow cast by the branches. Wiley's clothes hung loose, and his skin was pale and paper-thin.

They stood hip to hip, raised their hands and placed them on the bark.

"The Old Y gives us another day," Wiley said.

He could feel the rough ridges beneath his palms, twisted like basketry. The trunk smelled like a wood fire recently quenched. A bird *churred*, another *tinked*.

"Sapwood, heartwood," Wiley intoned. "One life, one center."

She lifted her hand and set it on his. "As strong as ever."

Wiley faced her. Her cheeks and brow were golden brown, and her large brown eyes were wide. She laughed and they softened, waving their feathery lashes.

"Nadja," he sighed.

How many more mornings like this, he thought, would they walk the canyon, trying to warm his bones in the winter sun? All life's gifts, its treasured sensations, earthly, inconsequential— Her calves' tapering sleekness. The ineffable lightness of her step. The musical lilt of her voice. Her delicate fingers— And now the clasp, firm and reassuring.

Nadja helped him over the Old Y's roots, retrieved his stick, and they started back along the trail.

The banks of the stream were brick red, and the water glittered like an aisle runner woven with jewels. The path was red too, and it wound between spans of fallen redrock. Wavelets *chucked*, finches *cheeped* from the shrubs, and a collared lizard did push-ups on a slab as they passed. The cliff rose from the opposite bank, redrock blocky and bulging, divided by vertical cracks. Its castellated heights looked like ramparts.

As they rounded the bend, a lone climber appeared. He was dressed in blue fleece, halfway up the cliff, following a seam.

"Scaling the walls of Zion," Wiley said.

As the trail descended, the valley broadened; the cliff receded and the stream's banks laid back.

The way led through a stand of velvet ash, and the leafless branches were drooping with wafery seeds. Nadja skinned a handful from a twig and halted. Wiley did the same. Together they gave the seeds to the breeze, watching them fly a few yards and settle on the stream.

She squinted into the sun, then she turned and squinted at him. "Are you tired?"

"No," Wiley said.

So Nadja held the scrub aside, and they left the trail.

They struggled up a modest slope and traversed the bank till they reached a discolored block. Wiley removed the knife from the sheath on his hip. The blade was tarnished and pitted. He sank to his knees. Nadja watched.

The block had a diagonal groove, and Wiley moved his knife into it, using the point to chip away rock. The groove was scarred where the blade had dug on mornings past. After an interval of patient carving, Wiley removed an object the size of a hazelnut and put it in his coat pocket. "It's the last," he said.

Nadja helped him rise, and they headed down the slope. As they reached the trail, the alert on Nadja's phone sounded. She drew it from her pocket.

"Right on time," she said. "He's on his way from the airport."

"Good with directions."

Nadja saw the humor in his comment, then caught herself, eyeing him with suspicion. "He knows what to expect?"

Wiley made an innocent face, a smile lurking.

Around another bend, a branch in the trail appeared. A path lined with small rocks climbed the slope. As the couple ascended, a wing of the stone refuge appeared. Then both were visible, large and two-storied, projecting on either side of a central structure with a rosette window and gable roof.

Though Wiley knew his visitor from messages, phone calls and a long video conversation, this first in-person meeting would be challenging. There was a lot to disclose, and the man would be surprised. Be ready for that, Wiley told himself.

They passed through the orchard, a grove of small trees with empty crowns, standing among the withered grasses. Farther, the gardens appeared. The plots were winter-blown. Amid the remains of autumn asters, someone had planted a white crucifix. It was waist-high, and its slats were battered.

Keep the financial reward in view, Wiley thought. And the glory of the prize—that will matter to him. As they climbed the stair to the patio, Wiley reviewed the things he was going to discuss, and the order in which he would discuss them.

He opened the French doors, and they entered, moving through a sun room with potted plants, carefully tended. They passed a sitting area with a fireplace built of river rocks, stepped down a hall paneled with burgundy wood, and paused before a doorway. The door was half open.

"Beautiful morning," Greven smiled, waving them into his office. "You have something for me?" He peered through his horn-rimmed glasses, looking trim and cheerful in his white lab coat and bow tie. The part in his black hair was perfectly straight.

"I do," Wiley said, reaching into his pocket, charmed as always by the doctor's dapper manner. He was like a tightrope walker with a top hat and umbrella.

The office had a woven rug, raised wainscoting and a broad window facing the highway. Greven stepped from behind his desk as the couple approached.

Wiley held the object he'd carved out of the rock and turned it before Greven's eyes. For as little time as they'd spent together, they might have been boyhood friends.

Beside his desk was a large display case. Greven opened the glass door. The shelves were crowded with fossils and Egyptian artifacts.

"You do the honors," Greven said.

Wiley stooped and added the vertebra to the end of the reptile's spine. On one side of the spine were two carved jars, and on the other was a statuette of Anubis. The god's keen eyes peered out of a jackal's head, and his hands were extended, palms down, to calm whoever had come before him.

"He's here," Nadja said.

She was at the window, looking out. Wiley closed the glass door and stepped beside her.

A black pickup truck was turning into the gravel lot. Despite the winter chill, the cab window was down and a man's bare arm hung out. The truck passed a half-dozen parked cars facing the building, reached the lot's corner and stopped.

The cab door opened and a man sprang out, his sandy curls jouncing like coiled springs. He gazed at the stone building, fished in his back pocket and retrieved a scrap of paper, checking the address. Nadja glanced at Wiley. The man faced the building again with a puzzled expression. Then he slapped the dust from his jeans and started forward. He was average height, but his carriage belonged to a larger man. He swayed from side to side as he walked, as if he was used to uneven ground. Not yet forty, Wiley guessed. In the prime of life.

"That's Roan?" Greven asked.

"Let's go," Wiley said.

As the three of them reached the entry, the chime sounded. Greven took hold of the iron grip and swung the door wide.

Roan stood on the threshold, looking from the door—a dozen feet tall, carved with crests and shields—to the man in the white coat.

"I'm Dr. Greven." The doctor extended his hand.

Roan spotted the name badge on Greven's chest pocket. He shook the doctor's hand, lip snagged by a silent laugh, wondering at his circumstance. He could see the couple standing a few feet behind the doctor.

"I'm here to see Wiley."

"Of course." Greven motioned Roan to enter, passing him a clipboard and a pen. "I wanted to welcome you and introduce myself."

Roan wrote on the visitors' log.

"Feel free to enjoy the grounds while you're here," Greven said. "Our backyard's a sight." He smiled, looked at Wiley and Nadja, and retreated.

They stepped forward together.

"Recognize me?" Wiley said. He took Roan's hand. The fingers were calloused, knobby as ginger roots. "This is Nadja."

When Roan offered Nadja his hand, he averted his face.

"We've just come from the canyon," Wiley said. "You know the rock?"

"The Kayenta Formation. I thought this was your home."

"It is," Wiley said.

Roan's crow's-feet trenched as he looked around. The entry was paneled and lit by a chandelier with faceted crystals. To one side a wide staircase rose, its banisters draped with native tapestries.

"Shall we?" Wiley motioned.

Roan laughed and shook his head.

They stepped through the lobby and down the hall. There was an oxygen tank on a metal dolly, and a nurse in a white uniform was exiting one doorway and entering another.

"You've been ill?" Roan said.

Wiley nodded.

"Have you been here long?"

"This is a hospice, Mr. Roan. No one is here for long."

Roan regarded him. His lips parted, but nothing emerged. His eyes were mismatched, Wiley saw. They were both sage green, but one had an iris spoked with gold. "We'll talk in the library."

They proceeded down the hall, past three closed doors, into a room with books on shelves, floor to ceiling.

Nadja settled Wiley into a chair and laid the walking stick beside him. Then she removed her shawl and draped it over his thighs. Wiley kissed her cheek, and she returned the kiss. He's watching, Wiley saw, thinking her lips were too ripe for an old man like him.

Nadja turned to depart. Wiley motioned Roan into the chair across from him.

"This is what life does." Wiley spread his arms. "I'm proof there is no escape." He smiled. "Thanks for coming."

As Roan seated himself, Wiley saw him eyeing his old hands. They were liver-spotted and spindly.

"Sorry for the delay," Roan said. "There was a quarantine in Jakarta. A diphtheria outbreak."

Wiley waved the information away.

"I took my travel out of the deposit you sent me," Roan said.

"Fine." Wiley reached into his shirt pocket, feeling for the waterworn rock. The cold air had chilled it.

When he opened his hand, Roan saw it, like a thick finger and about as long. Wiley passed it to him.

The fragment was polished on one side, and it was there you could see the embedded orbs. There were five of them, each the size of a small pearl. As Roan turned it, the light caught hints of purple and red, green and gold. Wiley watched him run his thumbnail across the orbs. The polish exposed their concentric rings.

"The photos you sent," Roan said, "don't do it justice. But I'll stand by my guess. It's chalcedony. Both the orbs and the matrix look agatized. The reds are iron oxides. The plasma, the greens, are probably amphibole or chlorite."

"I'm not interested in the chemistry," Wiley said.

Roan read his irritation, but he didn't react. "The orbs look like they're sealed in the matrix."

"They do look like that, don't they. You're a master of calm. Are you being cagey with me?" The last he said with some humor.

"I've seen rare gems before."

"Not like these."

"No," Roan relented. "I told you on the phone. The orbs would be new to the trade. They're unique. I wouldn't have flown halfway around the world if they weren't."

Wiley leaned forward. "Straight talk. I'm an impatient man. You understand."

"Maybe I will, once you've explained." Roan handed the fragment back. "Now that I'm here, are you going to tell me where it came from?"

Wiley smoothed the shawl and set the rock on it. Then he reached inside his coat for a mylar envelope and removed a folded paper, dog-eared and grease-stained. It was yellow and brittle after thirty years.

"A small cove on a roadless peninsula," he said. "On the northwestern coast of an island in the Indian Ocean."

"You found it there?" Roan glanced at the fragment.

"It was given to me by a friend. I lived on the island."

Roan was silent, waiting.

"I worked for a local collective. We exported raffia and cotton. My friend made his living the way you do. He dug things out of the earth."

Wiley caught Roan's eye and held it. "My friend—Craag was his name—had a trunkful of rocks like this. He found the vein they came from. But he died before he could mine it." He offered Roan the folded paper. Roan took it. "The samples Craag collected— They vanished. All but this one."

"Stolen?" Roan unfolded the paper.

"There was a coup," Wiley explained. "They burnt the capitol and bombed the bridges. The new regime took every-thing Craag had. The *vazahas*—strangers—had to leave. That was thirty years ago. I never returned."

"Thirty years?" Roan lay the map on his thighs.

The land was tan colored, and the sea was blue. A peninsula jutted out, and its coastline had a divot with an arrow pointing to it.

"Vato Cove," Wiley said.

"You've been there?"

"No." Wiley shook his head.

"You have a claim?"

"There's no time for that. The government's a mess. A claim could take months, and I'm not sure we'd get one."

"Is the country stable?"

"A strongman's in power, but there are riots in the capital and soldiers with machine guns on every corner. The orbs can't go through customs. That means some kind of charter."

"The operation would be in secret," Roan said, "and illegal."

Wiley nodded.

Roan looked around the room. The shelves had been treated recently, and the terpene odor was thick.

"Mining," Roan said, "takes a team, equipment, provisions, vehicles. It's hard to do that on the sly." His brows lifted. "I'm sorry. If we'd had this discussion earlier, I wouldn't have come." He refolded the map.

"You're the right man for this," Wiley insisted.

"You're mistaken." Roan was handing the map back.

Wiley refused to take it. "You know gems. You've worked at the ocean's edge. And you do things your way."

Roan cocked his head.

"That's what they say," Wiley went on. "'A gambler. A hotshot. He crashed a plane to be first in Mongolia. He fought pirates getting opals out of Peru.'"

Roan laughed. "Look—your prospect isn't promising. It's based on hearsay thirty years old. Even if the trail was fresh, and you had a claim and a plan that made sense, I'd be a bad choice. I've never been to that part of the world." He came forward in his chair. "I've got a job in Brazil that will take my summer. Maybe in August—"

"I'll be dead by then."

Roan made no reply.

Wiley met his gaze. The younger man foundered in the silence.

"Your time commitment would be brief," Wiley said. "Find the orbs, bring them back; be available until you're no longer needed, or until I've passed."

"A venture like this isn't cheap."

"Whatever it costs," Wiley said, "it's worth it to me." He lifted the fragment. "What price would you put on a river of them?"

"I'm no fool for treasure," Roan said.

"It's a treasure like none on earth. There are five orbs in that fragment. I've seen pieces with hundreds, densely packed."

"How many do you—"

"Thousands, millions," Wiley's hand flew open. "More than you can imagine."

"You've never seen them."

"The man who discovered them did."

24

"Mining the surf line's a nightmare," Roan exhaled. "Slow, hard, dangerous."

Wiley let the quiet settle around them.

Finally Roan cleared his throat. "When a job is this speculative—"

"You can keep the rocks," Wiley said. "Every orb you find."

Roan stared at him.

"They'll be yours when I'm dead," Wiley told him. "I'll put it in my will. Whatever you bring back, I'll leave to you."

Roan was speechless, utterly confused.

"That's a fair reward for finding them at my expense. Don't you think?"

Roan nodded slowly. "If there are as many as you say. They'd make a big splash in the gem markets. But— If you're going to—" He was trying to soften his words. "If you're going to die. And you're offering to leave the orbs to me— Why are you so determined to find them?"

"I want you on a plane in forty-eight hours," Wiley said.

Roan's eyes narrowed. He's wondering, Wiley thought, if I'm in my right mind.

"Forget about everything else," Wiley said. "This is your purpose. Just this."

"Who lives there? What's the language?"

"A local tongue."

"Any English?"

"They do better with French. You worked in Haiti."

"I did," Roan said.

"With luck, you'll beat the monsoon." Wiley felt a surge of energy. He was still a man of passion and action; his mind was sharp, and his eyes were clear. Surely Roan saw that. The sentence of death was upon him, but the noose hadn't yet tightened around his neck.

Roan shook his head. "Why?" he asked again.

"Those orbs," Wiley looked at the fragment, "are drops that fell from God's fingertips."

Wiley's room was on the ground level. The headboard of his bed was against the interior wall, and the window gave a sweeping view of the cliff and the river. The floor was covered with pile carpet, ivory colored and soft underfoot. Pine sprigs and cones lay on the dresser and nightstand, scenting the air. On the chair by the bed was a quilt woven with gold thread.

Nadja helped him remove his coat. Then she braced his arm as he eased himself onto the bed. When his back was against the pillows, she unlaced his shoes.

"Don't worry," she said.

"Just when I think, 'He's with me,' I lose him. He's a doubting man."

"Your intensity frightens him." Nadja's voice was soft, but she spoke with British precision, every word fully formed.

Wiley shook his head. "He distrusts me, but it's more than that. He's at odds with life. He's divorced himself. It's strange,

26

but— If I'd met him when I was younger, I might have been drawn to him. And he to me."

"You're not as similar as you think," Nadja said. "You've been connected to people all your life. Roan is alone. And he isn't comfortable with women."

Wiley regarded her. "He couldn't look you in the eye."

Nadja retrieved a remote control and clicked it. A motor hummed and the bed rose, halting at the level of her waist.

"I wanted to give him the whole story," Wiley said, "but I didn't."

"That's probably best."

"What are you doing?"

"Combing your hair with my fingers," Nadja said.

"I'm taking a nap. Why do you care?"

"I want you to look good in your dreams," she laughed. "It's wonderful hair, thick and healthy—"

He caught her hand and kissed it. "All those years—"

"Let's not—"

"I had my strength," he said, "and so much time. I would have found them."

"Yes. You would have."

For a moment he was back in the warehouse, staring at the packing trunk. Had he closed the lid before the emergency van arrived? He had returned for the orbs after Craag's body was gone. Hadn't he? He remembered standing in the road by the warehouse the following night, nerving himself to go in. He could have hauled the trunk away. No one knew it existed, except the boy who'd discovered the orbs. The nameless boy.

Five years later, every shack on that road had been pulled down. Someone had taken the trunk. But who? Where was it now? In a thief's closet? In an army bunker or a ministry basement? Did they have any idea what the orbs were?

"You're tormenting yourself," Nadja guessed.

"It would have been so easy."

"You were smart," Nadja said. "You got out alive."

"And then I let three decades pass. Not so smart."

There was sufferance in Nadja's eyes, but he couldn't share it. "I could have walked that shore. Surprised them where they live. I could have lifted them out of the earth with my own hands."

"I don't think you should worry about Roan," Nadja said. "I saw the way he looked at that rock. I know that look."

They filled the silence with their separate thoughts.

Wiley's comfort came from the orbs, his only hope. They'd been his only hope since that day in the clinic. It was etched in his mind—the naked walls, the sterile rooms and echoing halls. After days of scans and biopsies, they received the diagnosis together. Nadja held his hand while the oncologist delivered the blow. That same night, Wiley dreamt that it was he who the orbs had carried away; it was his life they grieved and his rapture they sought.

"They were with me last night," he said. "The orbs lifted me. The joy, the bliss—I could feel it inside me. There was light pouring out of my eyes."

Nadja stroked his brow.

"I was like some holy creature," he said. "A martyr or a saint. I was an angel who'd walked the earth, and the creator was taking me back. I had a future that didn't depend on my failing body. To the orbs, I was still precious."

"You're still precious to me," she said.

"Craag was there, below me, seeing me off. 'Your time on earth has ended,' he said. 'Your life with them is beginning.'"

"Shall I open the window?" Nadja asked.

"Sure."

His ears followed her. The settle of her shoes, the *whisk* of her skirt, the *clink* of New Delhi bangles on her wrists. She was music to him, she was rhythm and life. As the window opened, a towhee called from the slope below the orchard.

"You know what Dr. Greven told me?" Nadja stepped back to the bed. "They're going to have fireworks in the canyon. They launch them from the river."

"When is this?"

"July fourth, you dunce." Nadja tapped his head with her finger.

Wiley grasped her wrist and pulled, gently.

She sank onto the bed beside him.

"Independence Day," he said softly, looking into her eyes.

Tears welled where her lashes met.

"Please," she whispered. "Don't say that."

29

Twenty minutes later, Nadja was seated in the chair by the bed, turning a page of the book in her lap.

Wiley was on his side beneath the covers, sleeping, breathing peacefully.

Dreaming of the orbs.

They were in another dimension—their home, their native space. An ethereal place, a fluid medium as translucent as they were.

Not a mob of them. Just a few. Pale and drifting. Perfectly round.

He had never seen them like this before.

They had a purple tint, a different hue than they did on earth.

The movements of each seemed random at first. But as you observed them, you quickly perceived they weren't independent. They had an affinity for each other. Each was faithful to its own impulse, but as they drifted, they remained together.

As on earth, they were soft. Deformable, like sea jellies. When they touched each other, they wobbled and clung. The orbs had an energy, a unity and a purpose that was impossible for a human to comprehend. Even at close quarters.

They were mustering their energy for departure, Wiley thought. Or huddling, ticking to each other, making plans for him. Or . . . just floating in sleep, dreaming about him the way he dreamt about them.

2

"It's the time," Wiley said. "Time makes waiting impossible."

He was sitting up in bed, staring through the window at the immovable cliff. Nadja knelt on the bed beside him, a bowl of sudsy water in one hand, a razor in the other. "Hold still. I don't want to nick you."

"If I was there with him—"

"But you aren't." Nadja ran the razor down his cheek.

"I know—I have to trust him. But I can't help worrying about the problems he's having. And I don't think I'm hearing the half of it."

The day of his first meeting with Roan had been a long one. After Wiley's nap, the two men talked into the night. Nadja had been right about Roan, and in the late hours, the lure of the orbs prevailed. They'd signed the contract Wiley had ready.

They began making arrangements the following morning, and before the sun set, Roan was airborne to Africa. He'd reached the island under cover of darkness on a prop plane from Cape Town. In the coastal city of Jangaville, Roan called and Wiley shared his advice and cautions. Roan managed to find a foreman, purchase supplies, hire a team and rent two boats without raising suspicions. They left the port before dawn, unobserved by the authorities, and reached the Cove without any mishaps. After they'd set up their camp, they began digging pits.

Roan had a satellite phone, and they spoke daily, using a video link so Wiley could see what was going on. The eight black men dug, while Imran, the foreman, watched. They worked when the tide was low, at midday and in the middle of the night, shoveling sand and earth from the pits, abandoning them when the tide swept in. There was no mistake— they were in Vato Cove. But a week passed without any sign of the vein.

Then the conflicts over the sat phone began. Wiley had asked Roan to call every day, and at the outset he'd honored the request. But at the end of the second week, he resisted.

"My batteries are only good for three days," Roan said. "To recharge them, I have to board the cruiser. It takes a couple of hours and burns my gas."

"You're all I have," Wiley said.

"It's a waste of time. There's nothing to report."

Wiley could see the blue water behind him, he could hear the hiss of the surf. Over Roan's shoulder, a black man straightened and unloaded a shovelful of sand onto the beach.

"Be patient," Roan said, and he disconnected.

Roan's daily calls ceased, so Wiley made them himself. Sometimes Roan picked up, and sometimes he didn't. At the end of the third week, the two had it out.

"Do you want your orbs or don't you?" Roan said.

"Please. Humor me. I want to know—"

"One of the men found a floater," Roan said. "Badly weathered, the size of a dinner plate. A few orbs were visible. We're in the right place."

"How is Imran doing?" Wiley asked.

Roan sighed and mopped the rain from his brow.

In their first calls, Roan talked about how helpful the foreman was, but more recently he'd said nothing. When Wiley pressed him, he called Imran "a difficult character."

Roan was shaking his head. "I have to go."

And the line went dead.

After that, Wiley's calls went unanswered. Nadja advised him to stop, and he did. But the silence fed his fears.

"Let him do things his way," she said. "He'll call when there's news."

"Maybe tonight."

"Maybe tonight," she nodded.

The call came nine days later.

"We found it," Roan said, speaking loudly over the rain and the chirping frogs.

Wiley stared at the screen, waiting, speechless.

Roan's hair was wet and matted, his jaw unshaven. His brow dipped, then his hand appeared, holding an oblong rock the size of a baguette. As he turned it, orbs came into view. Scores of them, pearly and packed closely together.

"Good god," Wiley sighed.

Nadja gripped his arm. They were sitting shoulder to shoulder in the hospice dining room, with the screen on the table before them.

"This came from the water's edge," Roan said. "The vein is headed inland. All we have to do is follow it. We'll give it everything we can at low tide. Once we're higher on the beach, we may be able to run a full shift in daylight."

"How much have you mined?" Wiley asked.

"This is it, right now. There will be more the next time I call. I can't speak for the quality of the material. I'll know better once we've removed a few hundred pounds."

"How large do you think the vein is?" Wiley eyed the image of himself as he spoke. His blue eyes still had youth in them.

"No idea."

"Can you show me?" Wiley said. "I'd like to see it."

"Most of the vein's still buried. We have to trench around it."

"I wish I was there."

"No you don't," Roan muttered.

As Wiley watched, a scowl twisted Roan's mouth. This wasn't a man who'd just found a treasure.

"You look tired," Nadja said.

Roan nodded. "I could use some sleep. The rain won't let up. And the frogs—" His voice sank into the chirping throng. The sound was constant, like bad interference.

"—delirious," Roan's voice resurfaced. He swore and turned, avoiding the sat phone camera.

Something's wrong, Wiley thought, wrong with his words, wrong with his eyes.

"You're not on the beach," he said, raising his voice. There were trees behind Roan, and the leaves were dripping.

"I'm on the hill above, in the forest."

"How's your team?"

"Everything's fine."

"Tell me the truth," Wiley said.

Roan faced the camera. "Imran's gone."

"Where did he go?"

"Back to Jangaville, I suppose. He took the inflatable."

"Why?"

"Nonsense. Crazy fears. I'll sort it out."

Wiley drew closer to the screen. "I thought Imran was the only one who spoke French. How will you talk to them?"

"I said," Roan glared, "I'll sort it out."

The leaves behind Roan were moving. Wiley saw eyes, ghostly eyes, wide and watching. Lemurs, black and rust-colored, were descending the trees.

"I'll call you when I know more," Roan said.

"The monsoon's coming," Wiley warned.

But Roan had already disconnected.

They called Roan the next evening, and two days after that, but he didn't pick up. Wiley had lots of questions—they worried his waking hours and surfaced in sleep. He shared them with Nadja. He wanted to see the vein where it lay, he wanted to know its length and depth. That rocky baguette— He wanted to examine it closely. He wanted to see the mating surfaces, the spot where it had come loose. Had the orbs shown any signs of life? Roan had said nothing about that. What had he seen? And the men doing the digging— Did they know or suspect? They were there in the Cove, and he was ten thousand miles away.

Nadja did her best to calm him. They kept to their morning ritual, descending the slope behind the hospice, taking the trail below the cliff till they reached the Old Y. Two weeks passed without a word from Roan, and the walk grew harder. Wiley's legs were weakening. They quivered with every step he took. One morning they returned to find that they'd missed Roan's call. Wiley was upset and regretful.

They were able to connect with him that night, and the report seemed promising. He'd forged some kind of relationship with the oldest native, a man named Henri. Using props, sign language and a few words, the two were communicating.

With Henri's help, the dig was progressing. They were running two shifts. The men were strong, doing good work.

In four days and nights, Roan said, they had found the vein's limits. When it was fully exposed, the trench was a dozen feet wide and the depth of three men. They'd been taking rock for ten days now, using hammers and spikes. With every incoming tide, the sea brought sand back into the trench, but they were felling trees to build a dam.

When the call ended, Wiley was shaking. With Nadja beside him, they paced the vacant hall, talking, gazing through windows, lost in hopes and speculations. Wiley couldn't sleep that night, and the next morning his exhaustion caused them to put off their accustomed walk till after lunch.

His cane wasn't enough. He needed her sure arms every step of the way. As they approached the Old Y, the trail narrowed, winding sharply around the fallen rocks. As slowly as they went, Wiley's legs were still unsteady. His stick wobbled and his feet crawled. When they reached the Y, he couldn't get over the roots, even with Nadja's help. She put her hands on the tree and spoke the words while Wiley stood at the trail's end, silent. He couldn't stop himself—he was thinking of Roan, the vein and the Cove.

On the return, Wiley felt a new distance between them. Nadja said nothing, drawn into herself. She seemed unaware of the trouble her pace was causing. "Please, slow down," he said. And then, humiliated by his frailty, he put the lash to himself. It was that—the humiliation, the distraction, the mental gap that had opened between them—

As they rounded a bend, Wiley's ankle buckled. He fell onto his hip, groaning, breathless, cursing his body. Nadja tried to raise him, but his legs wouldn't take his weight. She did what she could to make him comfortable and ran for help.

That was the end of their walks to the Old Y.

When Wiley woke the next morning, his legs were so weak, he needed Nadja's help to get out of bed.

"Here's a good-looking one," Roan said. The camera eye was circling a small boulder. "Orbs on every side." His hand appeared on the rock, giving it scale, then drew back, directing Wiley's attention to the size of the pile. The speaker popped, the screen image froze, and when it returned, the pile was gone. Wiley could hear the waves crashing.

"He's done it," Nadja whispered. She lay on the bed beside him, arm at his back, holding him up. Roan had woken them. In the window at the screen's corner, Wiley saw himself, hair mussed, cheeks stubbled.

"We've started to cull them," Roan said, stepping to another pile. "These are lower quality. Poorly silicified. In some, no orbs are visible." Drops were falling now, and they dotted the rocks.

"How much have you taken?" Wiley asked.

"A ton and a half. Gem grade, maybe six hundred pounds."

The screen image stuttered as he moved.

"How much of the vein?"

"Twenty percent, I'd guess." Roan turned his camera eye, filling the screen with his face. "How are you doing?"

"I'm confined to the building now," Wiley said. Roan couldn't see the weight he'd lost, but his gaunt features were probably enough. His cheeks had hollowed. His lips had thinned and his jaw had shrunk. "I stumbled on the canyon trail."

"It was my fault," Nadja said. "We were rushing."

Their walks to the Old Y were over, and so were their strolls around the hospice—visits to the sun room or the fireplace, time in the library, discussions with Greven and the other residents. Wiley's life revolved around the orbs in the Cove.

"I'm ready to come back," Roan said.

Wiley searched the younger man's face. He looked worn, distracted. His lips lagged, and his gaze wandered.

"The monsoon's a deluge," Roan said. "The waves are too big. The dam can't handle them. The men—" He took a breath. "Their lives are at risk. We've got a good load."

Roan's image flexed. The speaker sputtered. Wiley stared at the screen. What was it? he wondered. More than Roan's weariness, more than the fear of physical harm. Wiley could sense the presence of something deeper, something arcane.

Roan's image stabilized. Was it rain that beaded his features, or sweat? Was he in some kind of fever? Roan raised his hand to wipe his face. It was brown with grime. His sage eyes lurched closer. The iris spoked with gold seemed to flash.

"I'm not sure how long I can hold this together," Roan said. "I'm—"

"No." Wiley came forward, making his eyes as large as Roan's. "I want it all."

Nadja grasped his shoulder.

Roan's face drew back. The next moment, it smeared. Had rain fallen on his camera eye? Roan's mouth distorted. His brow, his temple, his eyes—were swimming. Wiley could see his neck and shoulders, and the front of his chest. A spot of scarlet, the size of an orange— Blood was seeping through Roan's shirt.

"What is that?" Wiley said.

There was no reply.

Then the screen went dark. The call had ended.

Pushing Roan to stay changed things. Wiley worried about what he'd done. The dangers in the Cove— How threatened was he? Nadja was agitated too. They agreed that Wiley's craving for a blissful end didn't justify endangering others' lives.

He left his bed infrequently now, and only with Nadja's help. His concerns for Roan troubled him in the daylight hours, and at night they entered his dreams. In one, Roan was feverish, out of his head. He knelt before Wiley, grimy and shivering, sobbing and begging to come back to the States. But returning wouldn't help him now. He had crossed sanity's borderline.

Wiley woke, shaken. He didn't share the dream with Nadja. The next day, thankfully, Roan called again. There was no mention of returning. Pride sealed his lips, Wiley saw. And the strange spot of blood— Roan dismissed it. "An accident," he said, and he wouldn't say more.

Despite that, Wiley's ominous dreams continued.

Roan was on the rim of the trench, bossing. The natives halted and faced him as one, then they mounted the rim, raised their arms and fell on him together, attacking him with picks and spikes. Days had passed. The monsoon still raged, but the Cove was deserted. The trench was flooded now, and Roan's dismembered parts were floating in it. The natives had taken the rocks, returned in a boat to Jangaville and sold them all for a song.

Along with the fear for Roan's safety, the dream revealed another—that his obsession might be self-defeating. His desire to have all the orbs might cost him the chance to have any.

A week of fitful sleep, then a nightmare again. He dreamt that Nadja insisted on visiting the Old Y, despite his incapacity. They left the hospice in the dead of night, and somehow he made it down the slope without her help. She was a dozen yards ahead of him. Wiley hobbled around the bends on his own, falling and struggling back to his feet. Finally the end of the trail appeared. The natives were there, and the Old Y was no longer standing. The black men had chopped it down. They were crouched around a raging fire made of the tree's trunk and boughs. Roan was in the flames. They were roasting his body like a pig on a spit.

It was past midnight. The light on Wiley's dresser was lit. He was awake, sitting up in bed. He was hungry, and Nadja had gone to the kitchen to find him something to eat. Two weeks had passed since Roan's last call, and Wiley was expecting another soon. Maybe that night. The video screen and the dialer lay on the bed by his leg.

He picked up the dialer, then set it back down.

The calamities were imagined, he thought. Roan was fine. He had news, important news.

I should wait for Nadja, Wiley thought.

He stared at the dialer for a long moment. Then he grabbed it and made the call.

It rang once, twice, a third time— Roan didn't pick up.

I was wrong, Wiley thought. Not tonight. He put his thumb on the dialer to disconnect.

A snapping sound, then a buzz and the screen lit up.

An image appeared, like eels writhing in mud. It jittered and flashed, then slowly the image resolved. Wiley saw a black man's face. An old man, a man his age. His face was wet and dripping. His lips were thick, split and scabbed, and his nose was large. The man wore a ball cap, and his gray goatee was braided in strands that hung from his chin.

"Salama!" the man said, peering at Wiley.

"Put Roan on. Roan. Roan—"

Rain pelted against the black face with a noise like raked gravel. The image slid sideways, the old man vanished. Wiley saw a pant leg, a bare foot and a stretch of sand. Then the face loomed back, filling the screen, eyes narrow. "Dyeen man?" the black lips said.

"Roan. I want to talk to Roan."

The old face nodded. "Dyeen man."

A strange sound reached Wiley's ears. Rhythmic, forceful, like water churning. A throng of voices, rich with emotion. Chanting. The old man was turning, and the image turned with him.

Wiley was looking down from a prominence. The piles of orb rock came into view. Then he saw the trench and the men down in it. They were chopping with picks, swinging long-handled hammers. The wind whipped past, rain lashing their bodies, arms and chests and backs gleaming, stripped to the waist. Black, all black. All but one.

Roan's pale body moved with the rest, hammer lifting and powering down, expression bitter, his eyes raging, unintelligible grunts and bellows emerging from his lips. Beyond the far rim, Wiley saw the green walls, impossibly high, curling and crashing, threatening to flood the trench and drown the men.

"Fish eyes," a voice barked.

Wiley saw the old man's face rotate back into view. The

wind whipped his braided beard, and his scabbed lips smiled. "Fish eyes," he said, as if announcing some kind of celebration.

All at once, a torrent of rain poured down. The sky had opened up, and the old man was drowned. As Wiley watched, the image bobbled. Then it jarred abruptly. The connection broke, and the screen went blank. Only a mindless hissing remained.

The doorknob turned, and Nadja stepped into the room with a tray in her hand.

"What is it?" she said, seeing his bewildered expression.

Wiley shook his head, unable to speak.

After that, there were no more calls.

Wiley was climbing out of the trench with the others as the monsoon roared. Naked head to foot, they turned as one, waiting for Roan's directions. The deluge was heavy and warm.

Roan left the rim last. He shouted and waved his arm. Wiley dropped his spike, and all the men's digging tools fell to the ground. Roan faced Wiley, looking into his eyes with those sage beacons.

"The digging is done," he said.

Roan spoke with command, and he spoke the truth. The trench was an empty grave. "She awaits us," Roan said.

He motioned to the piles of orb rock that studded the hillocks.

She. Was it *she* then? That presence he craved. That holy mate.

Roan was leading, and they were following. They all knew Wiley's desire. Their hearts felt it, as if it was their own. And as they drew near, the piles smoothed or grew angular. One was a knee, one the wing of a hip or a thrust-back shoulder. An arm shifted. The head turned.

The random heaps were slipping together, and the reclining whole had structure and beauty. A woman, a maiden. The black men were chanting, and Wiley was too. The one they'd sought—the Maiden of the Orbs. She'd been waiting, ready but patient, and as they approached, she drew her legs in and rose.

Was the earth shrinking, or had Wiley grown?

The Maiden stood beside him now, shorter than he, but with a metal tub on her head. She was statuesque, barefoot, with a patterned wrap around her. She stepped forward, both hands free, tub perfectly balanced, hips shifting in time to the native voices. She had brown eyes, black skin and gleaming teeth, and her gait was buoyant, jaunty. An island woman, like any you'd see on the street or in an open-air market. But with a bounty that set her apart from every creature on earth.

Roan was beside him. As they followed the Maiden, Roan leaned closer, chanting louder, encouraging him. Wiley raised his voice, drawing from his heart, triumphant, exulting. He could see Roan's wound now, crusted and seeping, a hole the size of an orange. Around them, the natives were stumbling through the mud, still joined to the chanting. There was silver

45

light—from the stars, from a smear of moon—and it lit naked backs and limbs, and the Maiden in the midst.

Frogs hopped around her feet. Behind them, rivers of frogs were descending, pouring through the forests and over the hills. The black princess, the bearer of impossible gems, a gift rarely delivered, an answer to yearning so rarely fulfilled.

It was their mission to escort her across the deep.

As they reached the surf, tiny bulbed fingers gripped the rim of her tub, and a frog's head poked above it. Then the Maiden began to rise. She was floating over the curling waves, and the men were floating with her.

Orbs lifted from her tub, glittering, pulsing, concentered like eyes.

"Fish eyes," a man rasped in Wiley's ear.

It was Henri, the old native with the big nose and the braided goatee.

The tub was a pot of boiling fish, and their eyes rose with the steam. They turned in the air, gazing at Roan and Henri and the other men. And then Wiley felt them looking at him. Their concentered rings pulsed—

They peered into his soul. They knew who he was.

The orbs were for him.

Was Roan still with him? Or Henri or the men?

He was alone now with the Maiden and the rising orbs. Lifted invisibly, as if they were weightless, the eyes were dispersing on every side. They were borne away through the wind and the rain, and Wiley went with them.

3

Twelve days of silence followed the drowned satellite call. Then Roan sent a message from South Africa. He was on his way back with the rocks. Forty hours later, Nadja met him at the hospice threshold and escorted him to Wiley's room.

As the door opened, Wiley leaned forward, jarred by his heart, bracing himself with both hands on the bed. Roan appeared, stepping toward him, tousled hair, unironed shirt— The same man he'd met that first day. In one hand, Roan held a fist-sized rock.

"You're really here," Wiley said.

Roan extended his free hand, smiling. Wiley took it. Roan's grip was so firm, it hurt his fingers.

Roan set the rock in his lap. Wiley looked at it; then up, at the man's face, feeling dizzy. "Have a slice." He felt for the sheath knife on the tray beside him. With shaking hands, he carved a pear and held a piece out. Roan took it.

"I didn't dare believe—" Wiley's chest heaved, and a single sob rose in his throat. The testy renegade, this child of a man— He'd crossed oceans for him, caused him so much worry, had so many secrets— He'd risked his life to bring the orbs back.

"We're very grateful," Nadja said.

Wiley raised the rock in his lap. The blow of a spike had sheared it cleanly, and a mass of orbs crowded the mirror surface—hundreds of them. He reached for Roan's waist, circling it, drawing him close.

"The van's on its way," Roan said. "Where do you want them?"

"Here," Wiley said.

"In your room?"

Wiley saw the apprehension in his eyes. He thinks my mind is failing me, Wiley thought. He looked like he'd gained twenty years. His flesh was wan. His arms had withered. The bare leg emerging from the blanket had lost its calf.

"We were worried about you," Wiley said.

Roan nodded.

"You were able to control the men."

"Henri saved me," Roan said.

"I saw him. He picked up the last time I called."

Roan looked surprised. "The rain ruined that phone."

"I could see you with the natives," Wiley said. "In the trench. Things looked desperate."

48

"They were," Roan replied. "The monsoon was impossible. The trench kept flooding. We lost a man. He was swept out to sea."

Wiley's keenness faded. Nadja put her hand over her mouth. Roan bowed his head, unwilling to share his guilt. The dangers, Wiley thought, and his dreams— His fears had been real. "They stood by you," he said. "Even with that."

"Because of Henri. They were devoted beyond anything I could have expected."

"Why did he pick up my call?" Wiley asked.

"Trying to help, I suppose."

"He knew who I was," Wiley said. And then, "What are 'fish eyes?'"

That gave Roan a jolt. He shook his head, as if he didn't understand the question. Wiley watched him, waiting, feeling the pressure of the silence mount.

"Tell me," Wiley said.

Roan struggled to speak. The Cove had spooked him, Wiley thought.

"The orbs— They looked like fish eyes to him."

"You know," Wiley said softly.

"Know?"

The man had been intimate with the orbs, Wiley thought. He was discounting the things he'd seen, just as Wiley did thirty years before. What Roan knew was buried at the back of his mind now, bound up in doubts, smothered by reason.

"Was it difficult, bringing them back?" Nadja asked.

Roan shook his head. "The storms died, and the sun

49

came out. We ferried them through the surf and loaded them onto the cruiser. When we reached Jangaville, the pilot was waiting."

"You got them all?" Wiley asked.

"Every last one."

Rattles and squeals sounded in the hall. Someone knocked on the door.

The hem of Nadja's turquoise sari curled like surf as she crossed the carpet. She opened the door and stepped aside. A stocky man with jet black hair wheeled a hand truck loaded with crates into the room. Two others with trucks and crates followed.

"By the dresser. Beneath the window," Wiley pointed, showing where he wanted the rocks.

The man with black hair raised a pry bar and worked it beneath the lid of his topmost crate. A shriek sounded, and the lid rose. He passed the pry bar and began removing rocks. Roan bent to help him, and as he did, Wiley saw a white bandage beneath the neck of his shirt.

"What happened to your chest?" Nadja asked.

"A stupid move," Roan said. "The cut won't close."

More shrieks as crates were opened. Dr. Greven appeared in the doorway. He edged between two hand trucks and halted at the foot of the bed, eyeing the rocks on the floor.

"How many boxes are there?"

"Twenty-seven," Roan answered, lifting rocks out of a crate.

"There won't be space," Greven objected. "The floor won't take the load."

"It's a half ton of rough," Roan said. "Your floor can hold it."

"They won't be here long." Wiley spoke softly.

Greven sighed. "Your sister called again."

Once the rocks were uncrated, Wiley had a close look at each. In some, the orbs appeared on the surface, exposed by a fracture. In others, they bubbled in a pocket or massed in the depths. When he'd finished his examination, he asked Roan and his men to move his furniture to form a crescent around his bed. The dresser became part of it, then the desk, a lowboy and both of his nightstands. The surfaces were covered with towels, and Wiley had them pull the drawers halfway out. Then rocks were lifted onto them until they formed a cave around his bed. The two chairs remained where they were.

Roan stood beside the cave, with the view of the canyon behind him.

"Help me," Wiley asked Nadja, scooching to the mattress edge.

She wrapped her arms around him. Wiley clambered up her, and when he straightened, Nadja took a strap from the bedpost and bound her waist to his. Then she walked him around the bed, so he could scan the tiers of piled rock. He asked her to budge one and another. Roan signaled to one of his men, and the two of them helped rearrange the rocks so the thickest clusters of orbs were facing out. Nadja widened her stance and bent her knees to support Wiley's weight.

Finally, Wiley faced Roan. "Can we talk?"

Roan dismissed the men.

"I want you to lie down," Nadja said.

She led him back to the bed, removed the strap and eased him onto the mattress.

Wiley leaned back against the pillows, allowing his eyes to close for a moment. When he opened them, he felt calm and able. "Please—" He motioned Roan to a chair.

Wiley scanned the cave of rock as Roan sat down.

"They're exquisite," he said. "It's a miracle they're here."

Nadja posted herself at the foot of the bed.

"It's with a heart full of gratitude," Wiley went on, "that I'm going to say goodbye. But it's time."

He spoke with his old self-assurance. Roan seemed surprised by that. Or perhaps it was the finality in his words.

"You have your paperwork," Wiley said, "the title and so on. Nadja will make sure you're reimbursed for any unpaid expenses. From your perspective, is everything in order?"

Roan nodded.

"She tells me you've got a flight in a few hours, so I'll say my farewell now. I'm guessing you have some inkling of the gift you've given me. But I'm not going to press you."

Wiley showed Roan a glint of curiosity. Then he turned his attention back to the cave around him. "They'll be yours when I'm gone. You have plenty of time."

The room was silent and the drapes were drawn. Nadja lay on the bed beside Wiley. He clasped her hand.

"Tell Dr. Greven goodbye, and the nurses and attendants. Give them my thanks. I'd do it myself, but they wouldn't understand."

"Do you want me to call your sister?" Nadja asked.

"After I'm gone."

Wiley peered into the deep brown eyes. He drew a breath.

"I don't have any choice," he said. "You know that. If things had been different— We might have had twenty more years together."

He meant to comfort her, but there was no stifling his pain.

"I wish I could stay here with you," Wiley said.

The bliss awaiting him faded. All he could see was Nadja. The tip of her canine, her jugular notch, how her eyebrow narrowed to nothing as it completed its arc— A world of detail he had missed or ignored. Was he seeing her now as he should always have seen her? Or was this Nadja only visible through the magnifying lens of departure?

She was wearing the same sari, he realized. The one she wore the first time they'd met. She'd chosen it with care, eager to make a good impression on the trader her father held in such high esteem. She had given up too much to be with him, he thought. Their years together hadn't paid for the shattering news, the grim prognosis, the wasting weeks and months she'd endured.

She was reading his thoughts. He could see the care in her eyes and the reassurance: she hadn't given up anything, she was where she wanted to be.

"Don't worry about me," Nadja said.

Wiley kissed her hand. "Life could have been kinder."

"I'm thankful," she said.

He nodded and tried to smile, retreating back into the murky realm of his imagined departure. Without knowing how it would feel, or what Nadja would see, Wiley faced the orbs.

He cleared his throat. "I'm ready to leave."

Silence. Stillness.

Would they slide from the rocks, or bubble and gush? He could see Craag in his arms as the orbs gathered around them. When they bore him aloft, Wiley thought, would he see Nadja below? Would Craag be watching across the years?

His pulse throbbed in his temples. He held his breath, eyes on the cave, watching, waiting.

A minute passed. And another.

The orbs were motionless.

Wiley relaxed his gaze, exhaling, entrusting himself.

Another minute passed.

The orbs were still in the rocks, and he was still on the bed.

All his hope, Wiley thought. All the work— He felt spurned and abandoned.

Nothing had happened. Nothing at all.

Nadja burst into sobs. She threw her arms around him, furious, relieved, hugging him desperately, angry and helpless.

Two minutes later, she was standing by the window, facing the cliff, cellphone to her ear. "He has to speak with you," she said.

Wiley imagined what Roan was saying.

Nadja's eyes flashed and her nostrils flared. "He's going to make you a wealthy man. You can give him a few more minutes."

Her eyes shifted as Roan spoke. Then she ended the call.

"He's coming back," she said.

"I'm going to need more than a few minutes."

Nadja strode to the door, opened it and hurried out, leaving it ajar.

Wiley heard her footsteps fade down the hall. Somewhere to the north, between the hospice and the airport, Roan had slammed on the brakes. His car screeched to a halt by the side of the road. Wiley imagined him swearing, striking the wheel with the heels of his hands. Whatever had happened in the Cove, Wiley thought— Roan wanted to forget it.

The minutes passed quickly. Wiley wondered what the orbs needed from him, what they wanted— Craag's departure had seemed so effortless.

His thoughts were interrupted by Roan's voice, outside his door.

"There's nothing more I can do for him."

"He has so little time left," Nadja said.

"I'm going to Brazil. I made a promise, and I'm not going to break it."

"Give me their number," she said. "I'll explain."

"That's crazy."

Roan had been through a lot on their behalf, Wiley thought.

"Does a man's life matter so little?" Nadja said.

"Wiley isn't dying because of me," Roan replied.

The door swung wide and Roan stepped forward, approaching the foot of the bed. "What is it?" he said.

Wiley looked at the cave of orb rocks. "You brought them out of the earth. You were with them every day." He motioned him closer. "I want to know what you learned."

"About what?"

Wiley studied him. "The orbs are alive."

Roan's lips parted. His lids winced. Was he feigning surprise?

"You know that," Wiley said. "You saw it."

Roan glanced at Nadja. Her face was expressionless.

"Closer," Wiley insisted, motioning.

Hesitant, guarded, Roan approached the headboard.

"Is it possible," Wiley said, "that death is a greater treasure than life? Something worth leaving the world for? That's why you went to Vato Cove. That's why the orbs are here."

"Look—" Roan shook his head.

"Whatever you saw," Wiley said, "whatever you felt— The orbs will be yours. You need to know what they are. Craag— The man who found the Cove, the man who gave me the map and the fragment—"

Wiley leaned forward and extended his hand.

Roan stared at it. Reluctantly, he grasped it.

"I was with him," Wiley said, "the night he died. The orbs carried him away."

Roan flinched as if something had stung him.

The fish eyes, Wiley thought. Was he seeing Roan through the filter of dream, or was Roan remembering?

It wasn't a fever, Wiley spoke to Roan in his head. *It wasn't delirium.*

Roan bit his lip, denying. But Wiley was seeing Roan on the beach, with the fish eyes floating around him.

"I want a death like Craag's," he said. "I want to go where he went, feel what he felt." He pulled on Roan's arm. "Sit here beside me. I'm going to tell you what I saw that night."

Roan agreed to stay for a couple of days. He called his clients and rescheduled his flight. Nadja thought he was acting out of sympathy, but Wiley believed there was more. The story of Craag's blissful passage had touched him, Wiley thought. Roan knew something about the magic of the orbs, and a part of him—buried, in eclipse perhaps—was in tune with what Wiley had told him.

"The challenge," Wiley said, scanning the tiers of rocks surrounding his bed, "is to understand what triggered the moment."

Roan stood listening, arms folded across his chest. Nadja had left them alone.

"I thought his words had done it," Wiley explained, "that he'd brought them to life by accident. But— If that wasn't it, what caused them to leave the rock? What drew them to Craag? Was there something about the place or the night, or him?"

Roan followed his eyes to the motionless orbs.

"Let's put them in different positions," Wiley said.

He asked Roan to rearrange the rocks, placing the ones with densely packed orbs at the bottom, and those with orbs that were looser and freer on top. Then they adjusted them so there was more space between—space for the orbs to float into. Wiley tried to match the patterns he'd seen when the bubbling mass bore Craag away. But the orbs remained lifeless in every grouping he tried.

"I want to duplicate the conditions in the warehouse," Wiley said. "Get Greven."

Wiley explained the situation, and after a little cajoling, Greven volunteered that there was a trunk in the hospice attic. At Wiley's direction, Roan and the doctor moved the furniture, placing the trunk at the center. Then they loaded it with rocks. Roan was closing it, when Wiley stopped him. "The lid should be open."

Next Wiley focused on the windows. A breeze had been blowing through the warehouse transom when the orbs rose from the trunk. Wiley had Nadja open the casements, and the two men moved rocks and furniture again, putting orbs in the path of the draft.

Then a thorny issue. The night Craag died, there was a full moon.

"It's a crescent tonight," Nadja said. "The moon will be full in twelve days."

"I may not be here."

"Some moonlight might be enough," she said.

Wiley had dinner with her and Roan. Darkness was falling. Halfway through the meal, Wiley set his fork down.

"Let me try this with Roan," he told Nadja.

She left the two men alone.

The windows were open. The sky was clear. As the crescent moon rose above the cliff, its silver light touched the orbs in the trunk.

Wiley put his hand on the mattress beside him. "Would you mind?"

Roan seated himself on the bed. Wiley positioned him so he was as close as he'd been to Craag. He checked the time, then he made the pronouncement.

"I'm ready to leave," he told Roan, using Craag's defeated tone.

The orbs didn't respond.

Wiley waited and tried again. And again and again.

At 2 a.m., a fog descended, hiding the moon. They were far past the hour when the orbs had carried Craag off. Roan rose from the bed and went to the window.

"What are you thinking?" Wiley asked.

Roan was looking through the glass. "There's a fox," he said, "following the river. I can see his silhouette." And then, "They don't seem to care."

Roan spoke as if the failure was a triumph for the rational world. He's relieved, Wiley thought. Roan was back in the States, and it seemed the orbs were nothing but lifeless gems.

He turned, and Wiley saw the gloom in his eyes. Roan was sorry for him.

Wiley was sitting up in bed, staring at the cave of rocks. Roan stood to one side, watching. His failure with the orbs had left Wiley weaker. He'd feel a burst of energy, and then he'd sleep. There were knots in his legs and a piercing in his belly. Nadja and the nurses pestered him constantly with pain pills.

"Why are you doing this?" Wiley reached for the orbs, curling his thin fingers to coax them out.

Nadja got up, crossed the carpet quietly and left the room.

He turned to Roan. "When the spikes went in and the rocks came loose— When you lifted them out of the trench—"

Roan gazed at him.

"They were aware of what you were doing," Wiley said. "They reacted."

Roan shook his head.

"You're afraid of them, aren't you," Wiley said.

"It wasn't like that."

"They know we're here."

Roan raised his brows. "If you say so."

"Help me," Wiley begged him.

Roan shrugged. "Henri thought they could see."

"Fish eyes," Wiley muttered, wondering what it meant, how he might use the knowledge. He looked at Roan. "Certain thoughts, certain emotions attract them. There's something they need to see, to hear or feel."

Roan was silent. Then, in a muted voice, "You're like a half-dead coyote digging with both paws for a seep of water."

As much as the words hurt him, Wiley couldn't deny them. "I'm failing the test."

"Maybe Craag was a fluke," Roan said. "Their miracle wasn't intended for us."

"They don't know I'm here," Wiley said. "That's what's wrong. They can't see me or hear me." As the thought left his lips, he moved his breakfast tray to the side. "They need to be closer. We're going to put them right up against me."

An hour later, he was nested in rocks. Orbs touched his body at every angle.

Roan pushed a chunk against his ribs. "No more. The bedframe will go."

"Can you feel me?" Wiley asked the orbs.

Roan straightened, observing him with a dubious eye.

Wiley sent his need—his craving, his dire frustration—into the cold fragments hugging his flesh, and to those piled on the floor and drawers and dresser top too. Seconds passed, silent seconds. The orbs remained frozen in their glassy matrix.

An inspiration struck him. "They smelled the cut," he said. "They sensed his pain. Damage, weakness—"

On his breakfast tray was an apple, and beside it, his sheath knife.

Wiley grabbed the haft, drew his right leg from between the rocks and drove the tarnished blade into his shin.

Roan lunged, grabbed his wrist and wrested the knife from his hand.

His eyes drilled into Wiley's, angry, bewildered.

Blood was trickling from Wiley's leg, puddling around the rocks.

Roan wheeled and opened the door, stepping into the hall. "Where's the doctor?" he shouted.

Wiley watched Greven put in the last of the stitches. A nurse stood at his elbow with dressings and antiseptics. Roan removed the last of the rocks from his bed.

"I want Nadja," Wiley said.

"She's on her way," the nurse told him.

Greven glanced at Roan. "He's not giving up on his orbs."

"No," Roan said. "It's getting worse."

"I'm here," Wiley laughed. "You can talk to me."

Greven nodded at the nurse, and she made ready a bandage for the sutured wound. "I don't want you to injure yourself," the doctor said.

The door opened. Another nurse appeared, with Nadja behind her.

Wiley smiled. Nadja stepped toward him, then froze as she saw the stitched flesh. There was disbelief in her face, then some mawkish emotion trembled her lips.

He reached out his hand for her, but she seemed not to notice. As the nurse applied the bandage, Nadja covered her face with her hands. Greven put his arm around her shoulders.

"It's nothing," Wiley said.

She was sobbing now, shaking her head. She couldn't face him.

Greven pursed his lips, regarding Wiley like a vexed schoolmarm. He took the blood-streaked knife from the bed and wrapped a towel around it.

"I won't live to see the cut heal," Wiley looked from Roan to the doctor.

Greven's features softened. He gripped Nadja's arm, then he spoke with resignation. "When the end is near, the body seems dispensable."

"How long does he have?" Nadja asked.

Greven exhaled.

"I want to know," she said.

Wiley watched the doctor's eyes settle on him.

"Two weeks is my guess," Greven said.

Nadja's sobs returned. Greven and the nurse escorted her out of the room. The door closed, and Wiley was alone with Roan.

"She's frightened," Roan said.

"So am I. Time's running out." Wiley put his hand on his injured leg. "This body isn't worth a thing to me now." He narrowed on Roan. "What about you? What are you afraid of? The orbs will be yours in a couple of weeks."

"I'm not thinking about—"

"I can feel your dread," Wiley said. "You're carrying it around like a cloud."

"You're imagining things."

"They're not just rocks," Wiley said.

"They're just rocks to me."

"How did you get that hole in your chest?" Wiley asked.

Roan shook his head.

"I want to know what happened in the Cove. The truth—" Wiley clenched his fists. "I need your help. Can't you see—"

Roan's stunned expression sent Wiley into himself. *Was he imagining things?* As his life floundered toward an end, was he drowning in his own dreams? Maybe Roan had no secrets.

The younger man's face was grave. His hand rose, touching his shirt front and the wound beneath.

"You want a knowledge none of us have," Roan said. "Your wish can't be fulfilled. I can't help you, and neither can Nadja."

"Your true mind," Wiley insisted. "Tell me please."

"The end is inconceivable. People believe in something beyond—heaven, paradise, a kingdom to come. They have to tell themselves something."

"The truth," Wiley implored him. "I'm begging you."

Roan stepped closer. He sat on the bed beside him.

"Part of me hates what you're doing," he confessed. "I condemn you. I laugh at you." Roan took a breath. "And part of me admires you. Your determination, your stubbornness— Your refusal to surrender."

Wiley peered into Roan's eyes. The one with golden spokes glittered in its depths.

"It must be hard," Roan said. "Every day. Every hour, every minute—"

"I don't need your pity," Wiley said. "I need you to help me with the orbs."

"They aren't responding."

"There's a reason," Wiley said.

Roan shook his head. "I've got a job in Brazil."

"No gems in the world are more important than these."

"I can't help you."

"You can," Wiley said, "and you promised you would. You agreed to stay until you're no longer needed, or until I die. It's in writing."

Roan stared at him.

"I've never doubted you," Wiley said. "You're a man of your word."

Minutes later Roan rose to leave. As he opened the door, an odd sight greeted them. A half-dozen chattering women were moving down the hall, escorting a hunched lady with white hair. She used a walker, and her arms were quivering. Her hair was crooked and her eyes were bagged, but she nodded and laughed as if everything was right with the world. Some of the women were older, some middle-aged; and behind, four girls followed. A teenager with green braces looked through the doorway and smiled as she passed.

"Your new neighbor," Roan said.

Wiley could hear the group filing into the room next door. And only a four-inch wall between, he thought. What would they think about his ordeal with the orbs?

Roan looked at him.

He too was struck by the difference, Wiley thought. Death was going to enter both rooms, but it would be harder for him.

A knock sounded on the door.

It opened and Greven stepped forward. He nodded to Roan and Nadja, then faced Wiley. "Your sister is here."

"My sister?"

"She's brought another family member with her," Greven said.

Roan stood. Nadja rose from the bed.

A minute later, Greven ushered the two visitors in.

An older woman in a dun summer suit, with gray hair plaited around her head like a diadem, extended her arms to Wiley. "There he is."

He smiled and raised his to return her embrace.

She eyed the cave of rocks and circled inside them to reach the bed. Then she stooped and hugged him.

"I can't believe this is happening," she whimpered in his ear.

"I was going to live forever," Wiley recalled.

"That's what you said."

He tipped his head. "You were right."

She clenched the muffler around her neck, holding back tears. She was happy to see him but devastated too. "Why didn't you—"

"Kandace," Wiley sighed. "What was there to say that wasn't said years ago?"

Kandace straightened herself and glanced at Nadja, then she turned to the man behind her.

"Sid," Wiley said. "What a surprise."

A tall man stepped forward. His head was narrow and he

carried it poorly, craning as if he mistrusted his feet.

"A not unwelcome one, I hope," Sid replied. "'A brother is born for a time of trouble.'"

"You're Nadja?" Kandace asked.

Nadja nodded. Wiley saw the surprise in her face.

"They resemble our father," Kandace explained.

Sid's eyes were blue, and his hairline was high, with receding indents on either side.

"I've asked for a copy of the test results," Kandace said. "Experts can disagree." She saw the bandage. "What's happened to your leg?"

"It's nothing," Wiley said. She was already acting as if she was in charge.

Kandace frowned at the rocks, turning to Greven. "What are these?"

The doctor nodded at Wiley.

"They're rocks," Wiley said.

"That I can see," she laughed.

"It's none of your affair," Wiley said.

Her lips parted. Kandace looked at Nadja and Greven, then back to Wiley. "What's the secret?"

"You wouldn't understand," Wiley said.

Kandace stared at him. "Try me."

Wiley stared back. Pores had opened on either side of her chin. Her jowls looked like they'd been stuck with pins.

"The orbs in these rocks are going to carry me away," he said.

Kandace studied him. Then she turned to Nadja, squint-ing.

"I'm going with them," Wiley told her.

Kandace looked at the rocks.

"The wound in my leg," Wiley said, "was my doing. I stabbed myself. I did it for them."

Sid's shoulders lifted, as if pulled by metal hangers. He looked startled. Kandace turned to Greven.

"We've taken the knife away from him," Greven assured her.

"What kind of place are you running here?"

"Please understand—" Greven molded the air with his hands.

Kandace faced Nadja. "You're supposed to be caring for him."

"I've never been better cared for," Wiley said.

Nadja put her hand on his shoulder. "This is what Wiley wants."

Greven bowed his head. "I'm going to let you work this out." He stepped toward the door.

Kandace looked at Wiley. "I'm getting a second opinion."

"We did that," Nadja said.

"There's someone I trust."

"However you can help," Nadja said, "will be greatly appreciated." She looked at Sid. "We should have met before now." She stepped forward and extended her hand.

Sid clasped it. "How long have you been together?" he

asked with a bob of apology for his sister's harshness.

"Three years," Nadja said. "Wiley knew my father."

"He never said a word about you," Kandace observed.

"Stop it," Wiley demanded.

"The last I heard," she went on, "Wiley was with a diplomatic attaché. Before that, it was a Viennese museum director."

"Your English is impeccable," Sid told Nadja.

"I attended boarding school in London."

"You've seen the world with him, I suppose," Kandace said. "My brother has spent a lifetime chasing the exotic."

"What's happened to your trading company?" Sid asked.

"Nadja found a buyer for it," Wiley replied.

"A difficult time." Sid spoke to Nadja with sympathy.

"We had employees on three continents," she told him. "When we got the bad news, everything changed. We couldn't think about business."

Sid looked from Nadja to Wiley. "I'm so sorry."

"Things are serious for us now," Nadja told him. "Trading was a happy life. His lightness and charm drew people to us." She looked at Wiley. "Death doesn't care about that. Good cheer won't stop it or slow its advance."

"He's lucky you're here," Sid said.

"I'm doing what I can," Nadja said.

Kandace scowled at the rocks and Wiley's leg. "We can see what you're doing."

Nadja bucked her chin, her eyes flaming. "When was the last time you spoke with him?"

70

"I took care of Wiley before you were born." Kandace faced Roan. "What's your role in all of this?"

"I found the rocks," Roan told her.

"The magic rocks," Kandace nodded. "You're a sorcerer, I suppose."

"I've been respecting his wishes."

"I'll bet," she said. "What's in it for you?"

Roan laughed.

"This is humorous?"

Roan shifted his gaze.

"I'm here, young man." Kandace jabbed her fingers between her breasts. "Not over there."

"I have a contract with your brother," Roan said.

"You don't care about him," Kandace swept the room. "No one here does."

4

"Nadja said you were up late last night." Sid sat in the chair beside Wiley's bed.

"With Roan," Wiley nodded. "Seeing if wind matters." He gazed through the window. "The moon is waxing." The orbs were glittering, pointed by the morning light.

"Death's never threatened me," Sid said.

"Later is better." Wiley faced him.

Sid was twenty years younger, and he'd grown up in a different home, with Dad's second wife. Wiley remembered a timid boy. Sid had always been cautious with his emotions and preferred it when others were cautious with theirs.

"But— I can understand," Sid looked down, "how death's approach would turn your attention away from the world." He smoothed his pant leg. "You know I'm a Christian."

"I'm recalling."

"Fear opened my eyes to faith." Sid winced, conscious perhaps of how stilted he sounded. He swallowed his embarrassment. "Faith in a higher power."

What do you want? Wiley wondered.

"Life is fragile," Sid said, "short, uncertain. We want to believe there is something more." His eyes shifted to either side. "I don't understand the orbs. But— If you're reaching beyond this mortal life— I understand that."

"Do you?"

Sid drew back. Then he saw the warmth in Wiley's eyes. "I wish we had talked about these things before."

"I wasn't thinking about them before." Fate had brought the curtain down on his life, Wiley thought. And fate had called him to Craag's warehouse.

"Why are you here?" Wiley asked.

Sid's mouth opened and shut like a fish out of water.

"We barely know each other," Wiley said.

Sid shook his head. "I feel guilty about that. Sad. And deprived." He struggled to speak. "I've lived my whole life in your shadow. I've been jealous, Wiley. I've had envy in my heart."

There was pleading in his blue eyes.

"I want to be your brother," Sid said.

Wiley sighed. "I'm glad you came."

Sid's lanky frame quivered, and his shoulders rose. It was gladness, Wiley saw.

"I want to know about the orbs," Sid said, "and I'd like to tell you what I believe."

The knob turned, and the door swung open.

Kandace stepped forward with a tray of food. "Hungry?"

She passed between the two men and set the tray on Wiley's lap.

Wiley waved his hand to refuse and ask her to leave. But Sid was curling in on himself, retreating.

"Are we cheering him up?" Kandace asked.

Sid nodded.

Kandace faced Wiley. "Let's put a fresh shirt on you." She motioned Sid to the closet. "Do you need another pillow?" She reached for one and plumped it. "You'll never guess who I bumped into last week."

Wiley leaned forward, and Kandace put the pillow behind him.

"Britta Sher," she said.

Sid handed her a shirt.

"She's doing well," Kandace said, unbuttoning his front. "Married, three beautiful children. Those were the good times."

Wiley stared at his sister. "What are you talking about?"

Kandace slid his shirt off.

"Britta broke my heart," Wiley said.

"Whose fault was that? You frightened her. Here, put your arm in."

"Everything frightened her," Wiley said.

"You were terrible." Kandace buttoned the shirt. "I could hear you out on the veranda. All that talk about jumping off the edge of the world."

Wiley laughed. "You'll never stop scolding me."

"That's not true."

Sid turned and left the room.

"We were always fighting," Wiley said.

"Not always," Kandace disagreed. "You changed. You broke up with Britta, and you sprouted wings."

"Britta had nothing to do with it. I needed my freedom."

"You deserted us. You went off on your 'great adventure.' I had to take care of Mom by myself."

"I'm sorry—"

"All I got from you was a check in the mail."

"You know that's not true." Wiley felt again the price for leaping, for flying, for stealing away. I left because I had to, he thought.

"She missed you, Wiley. Your absence hurt her, especially at the end."

He reached inside himself, finding the justification he'd forged when he was younger. *There is no human connection to which you owe your life.* If not then, what could he possibly owe Kandace now?

"That's better." She straightened his collar and looked around. "Pictures would cheer things up." She spoke as if it were a room to let. "There's not much space, with all these rocks."

"Nothing is more important to me."

"That's all the nurses talk about, Wiley. You and your orbs. You're a celebrity."

"You're a guest here," he said.

76

"Are you threatening me?"

He regarded her. "You've been in Greven's office?"

Kandace didn't reply.

"Maybe you noticed the glass case. There's a figurine of Anubis in it, the Egyptian god of the underworld."

Kandace rolled her eyes.

"The new arrivals appeared before him," Wiley said. "Each had a scroll with incantations, spells of transformation, that turned your soul into a bird or a plant or a star."

"Wiley—"

"The orbs are my scroll," he said. "I'm leaving, and that's how I'm going to go. Humor me if you have to."

"This is nuts," Kandace said.

"I'm dying. Are you going to help me?"

Kandace stared at the air between them, as if she stood on the threshold of some dangerous awareness and was determined not to pass through.

"You're not in your right mind, and you're a danger to yourself. I can't just say, 'It doesn't matter.'" She was mumbling, barely audible. "I've asked Greven— I want to see your Power of Attorney."

"I am voluntarily giving this Durable Power of Attorney and recognize that these powers will become effective as of the date of my incapacity."

Wiley refolded the document, set it aside and regarded those gathered around his bed—Sid, Kandace, Roan and the doctor. Nadja stood close, and when he looked at her, she put her hand on his shoulder.

He motioned at the rocks behind the observers.

"The orbs have the power to lighten my leaving," he said. "I believe that. If my faculties fail me, Nadja will take command. The decisions will fall to her. Does anyone here doubt what she will do?"

The room was silent. Then Kandace spoke.

"Nadja may protect your fantasy. But she's no different than the rest of us. She doesn't believe a word of it. She just lacks the courage to tell you."

Wiley considered his sister's words. "Kandace doubts your belief," he turned to Nadja, "and others may share her doubt. Let's clear things up for them, shall we?"

Nadja eyed him uncertainly.

"If my faculties fail me, will you let me keep my rocks?"

"Yes," she said.

"Why?" he asked.

Nadja glanced at Roan. He raised his brows with a wry smile. Kandace was working her jaws like a horse trying to dislodge its bit.

"Go ahead," Wiley said. "They want to know."

Greven was nodding to Nadja. *It's alright. Be honest*, his eyes seemed to say.

Nadja removed her hand from his shoulder. "I love him," she said. "I already miss him." Her lips crinkled.

"It was hard for him to tell me. He had a table reserved at an old hotel in the Chandni market. He was so distant, so serious— While we ate, he described what he'd seen the orbs do the night Craag died." She shook her head. "I didn't know what to think. Was it something he'd imagined? Was it the shock of his friend's death? Wiley wasn't sure. He couldn't make sense of it."

Wiley watched Nadja's lips meet and part as she spoke. As grave as the subject was, her voice was still musical, rounded and cadenced.

"What did the orbs mean to us?" she said. "For years they meant nothing.

"After the diagnosis in May, they became part of our lives. The idea of what they could do. Wiley dreamed about them. I did too. We knew nothing. A memory, thirty years in the past. The fragment Craag gave him. The five orbs inside it.

"It was all wishing, wishing death wouldn't be so cruel. Wishing that if there was no remedy and no returning, there might be a parting without despair. Something inspiring. Something hopeful."

She gazed at the four listeners and took a breath.

"I want Wiley to join his orbs, whatever it takes. What better end could I ask for?"

Greven smiled. There was something like wonder in Roan's stare. Kandace clutched Sid's arm.

Nadja turned to see his reaction. Wiley nodded to show he was pleased.

"The season of facts is behind us," she vowed. "The orbs

are real to Wiley, and they're real to me." Her eyes brimmed. "I need him, badly. But I can't keep him. He has to leave. If he wants to go with them, I'll quiet my heart. I'll loosen my hold." She steadied her voice and spoke to the orbs. "'Take him, please. He belongs to you.'"

After lunch, Wiley napped. In the late afternoon, they reassembled.

"I got my second opinion," Kandace said. "He agrees with the diagnosis." She held up a scrap of paper. "He mentioned some new treatments. Alpha-lactalbumin. It kills tumor cells. And inositol hexaphosphate—"

"Kandace," Wiley sighed.

There was capitulation in his sister's eyes.

"I'm out of time," he said.

Greven's hands were in his white coat. Nadja and Sid were silent. Roan stood at the cave's wingtip, watching.

"I respect your right," Kandace said, "to die your own way. But please— Just listen to me. I know what a bad end is like." She stepped closer.

"Mom imagined she was still married," Kandace said. "Dad was with us. And—" Her voice caught. She reached for Wiley's hand.

He took it, peering into his sister's eyes.

"She thought you were there," Kandace said. "At the last

hour, she came to her senses. Nothing she'd imagined was true. It was terrible."

She looked at the rocks. "Wiley, what if the orbs don't emerge? What if the rocks are useless? That's going to make going ten times worse."

Her words touched him. They touched Sid and Roan, as well. Wiley saw fear in Nadja's eyes.

"There are no rules for dying," Greven said. "Last year, we had a woman who refused to take pain medication. Her suffering was severe, but she believed that enduring what she endured was right."

The room was silent.

"There are people around you who love you," Kandace said.

Wiley felt her hand tighten on his.

"We're here to say goodbye," she said. "Now is the time to feel our connection, the connection we all need and want."

Wiley sighed. "Will you leave me alone with my sister?" he asked the others.

Greven led them out, and Nadja closed the door behind her.

"Three days ago," Wiley said, "before you got on the plane— What did you think would happen here? What did you expect?"

"You didn't even call to tell me," she said.

"If I hadn't cut myself," he stopped her. "If there weren't any rocks here. If the orbs had no claim on me—"

"I thought we'd be close again. Like we were."

"We were never—"

"You don't remember," she said sadly. "Three days ago, I thought, 'Wiley needs me. All our troubles will be forgotten. It will be like it was.'

"I'm realizing now— What you're doing with the orbs, and to Nadja, is the same thing you did to Mom and me, and poor Britta. You're jumping off the edge of the world, abandoning those who love you, hurting us all."

"Is that why you're here?" Wiley asked. "To tell me how much I've hurt you?"

"No," her chest quivered. She began to sob. "That's not why."

"I can't take your anger with me."

"That's not why," Kandace whimpered. "I swear, that's not why." She was speaking more to herself than to him. "I shouldn't have come. I just—"

Her lips were swollen. Her tears followed the runnels in her aging cheeks.

"I wanted to feel needed again. I was a good sister once. Really. I was."

Wiley and Nadja ate dinner together. After, she washed him. When he was dry, she helped him into his nightclothes. Then she sat beside him and combed his hair with her fingers, and while she combed, she spoke of the Old Y.

"A tree," Wiley acted confused.

"Oh yes," she said, playing along. "A special tree."

She put her lips to his ear. "You'll see it as we round the bend. There's a stream that pours out of the rock. It's been pouring for eons, digging that pool, polishing its sides. The Old Y chose this place to plant itself."

"You have an affection for it," Wiley said.

"A very strong affection. You see how tall it is, with its two giant boughs."

Nadja raised her arms and spread them. "It's majestic this time of year, when the leaves are out. Even on a summer day like this, it's cool in the shade of its crown. Step over the roots," she said. "Put your hands on the bark next to mine."

She extended her hands, palm out.

Wiley did the same.

"I can see why you're drawn here," he said.

"'The Old Y gives us another day.'" Her voice came gently. "He says that—the man I love. We come here together."

"Do you," Wiley murmured.

"He's more than a friend and a lover. He's my faith in the magic of life."

"That's a lot to ask of a man."

"Not this man." Her tone was droll. "In a few weeks, when the cliff is crowded with swallows, and the redrock is dripping with green, the Old Y's leaves will be big and heart-shaped. And— You see those vines, tangled in the branches like spider webs? That's wild grape. It uses the Old Y to reach the sun." She spoke with a yielding sadness. "There will be

83

grape leaves on the highest branches. They're smaller, but they have hearts too."

They floated together, feeling the cheer of the imagined summer.

Finally Wiley turned and gazed at the window.

"It's nearly dark," he said. "Get Roan for me, will you?"

That night was a difficult one for Wiley. Roan sat in the chair. Nadja lay sleeping on the bed beside him. In fits, he spoke to Roan about new things they might try to stir the orbs. Wiley's eyes never closed. He was watching the rocks, hoping to see some movement. It was past midnight when exhaustion set in. "I'm out of ideas," he said.

A few minutes later, he felt his pulse change. His breath was suddenly short. His heart missed beats, chugging like a car about to stall. His arms jerked, his legs stiffened. The alarm on the monitor beside his bed began to buzz.

Wiley exhaled in a burst. A sharp pain made him cry out.

Nadja shuddered and sat up.

He rolled toward her, arms crossed over his middle to protect himself, as if he was being attacked by an invisible assailant.

She grabbed hold of him.

Roan was on his feet. "I'll get the doc," he said, moving toward the door.

Nadja put a pillow on her lap and eased his head onto it. Wiley groaned with pain and fear. "I'm here," she whispered, stroking his temple.

It's over, he thought. A grim acceptance invaded him.

All at once, he felt damp. The air around him was dense and watery. Beyond the ragged edge of the cave, mist covered the window glass, and in the dark sky beyond, a hazy moon hung, flattened on one side.

The moon seemed to draw closer. Even as pain drove through his belly, he felt the milky glow on him. The kindly conjuring. The moon had watched over him when he entered the world. It was only right that it should appear when it was time to leave.

Wiley heard a familiar noise. The sound of a hundred nuts cracking. Moonlight poured through the window, glazing the rocks.

Pearly orbs were pulsing inside them. Coming to life.

Was it happening?

They weren't aware of him. Oh, but they were. Very aware.

Could they see him? Not just see. Not just hear and smell. The orbs were looking into his soul.

The pain, twisting his belly, stretching his bones, cramping his legs— Could the orbs feel that? They could, they could. They felt and they knew. The orbs were experts at pain, and rapture too.

Nadja was with him. Orbs were rising into the dimness behind her, dotting the air with light. They glowed, they pulsed, each concentered with hoops that widened like rings from a raindrop falling on a pool.

Nadja's face was enormous. Her lips were rolls of Suvin cotton, and her eyes were cradles of warmth. Wiley looked into them.

I'll miss these eyes, he thought. Of everything I'm leaving behind, I'll miss them the most.

The orbs were moving around Nadja's head. She seemed not to see them.

Free of the rock now, light as air, they floated toward him, knowing him, feeling his need.

"Thank you," he whispered.

They rubbered apart and together, clinging to each other, floating into the space between his face and Nadja's, jotting her features. Wiley imagined them touching him, taking hold.

"I'm ready to leave," he told them, speaking from his heart. This time they were listening.

Clusters of orbs obscured Nadja and the rumpled bed. They were settling onto him, pearly islets, like sea foam or tiny soap bubbles, glistering as they rode over his skin.

He could smell them now. Their scent was purple, regal, floral. When he opened his mouth, pearls landed on his lips and tongue. They were jittering, excited; like an alien kiss or a mouthful of bees.

He could feel the jittering on his neck, his chest, his right thigh.

They were chafing his skin. Abrading it.

Wiley raised his arm. It was covered with pearly foam. The orbs were creeping into it, rusking away the beads of his skin. Flesh-colored beads, salmon and peach. Then crimson and scarlet. It wasn't a pleasing feeling. It prickled, and then he felt pain.

He remembered the pocks in Craag's flesh, the pits and divots; the scarlet threads, the bloody shawl flowing out of Craag's body; and the scarlet orbs that came bubbling up. Wiley recoiled, feeling the raw spots.

He wasn't meat and bone. He was orbs, like they were. As the pearly orbs dug into him, his own orbs were coming loose.

Flesh- and blood-colored, they swirled up from his body in warm clouds. Like the pearls, his orbs pulsed and glowed, each with a rhythm of its own, rippling with concentered rings, like a pond's surface struck by a flurry of rain.

But his orbs were heavy and sightless, weighted with iron. His orbs had the odor of sulfur, and when they landed on his lips, they tasted metallic.

The red orbs billowed over him. The pearly orbs were attacking his body at every angle, softening his borders, bubbling and clicking, jittering as one. He was like cheese passing over a grater, and as the grating advanced, so did the pain. When he'd held Craag in his arms on the warehouse floor, he didn't know what the pearls were doing. Now he knew.

Wiley's orbs were leaving, freed from the body in which they'd been bedded. The bright orbs of flesh were no longer his. They were drifting away. I'm dissolving, he thought. But it wasn't bliss he felt. It was fear. The orbs were flaying him. It wasn't like this for Craag, was it?

"Help me," he rasped, feeling utterly alone.

Nadja was stooped over him, holding him close, reading the pain from his eyes. It wavered, submitting; then it twisted as the gougings went deeper, freeing flesh in gobbets. Pain, impossible pain—

Wiley's head shook. His hands fisted the sheets. Again he cried for help.

The room light snapped on.

Something gripped his arm. His shoulders were lifting. Nadja pulled away.

Wiley saw Greven's face, then a nurse, and Roan peering between them.

"Careful," the doctor barked. Wiley struggled, gagging. Had someone put their fingers down his throat?

"His blood pressure's declining," Greven said.

Wiley saw Kandace now, and Sid half dressed. Their features were rigid. Behind them, the curtains were parted and the light of the moon was beaming through.

Nadja was sobbing, mopping his face with a towel. Roan turned away.

A burning rose through Wiley's arm, into his chest, and the room went black.

Wiley opened his eyes to daylight. The night had ended. He heard whispers, foot sounds, a *clink* of metal or glass. I'm still here, he thought. He felt a mattress beneath him. He was curled on his side.

He could feel what the orbs had done. From his soles to his shoulders, his flesh was raw. The orbs had left off. He was relieved about that, but— Why am I here? he wondered. They hadn't borne him away.

He straightened his leg, and the movement shrieked through his nerves. Did they mean to make his death an ordeal? Where was the bliss he had thought they would bring?

A clothed hip appeared, then a face. Nadja, smiling, eyes deep.

"We thought we'd lost you," she said.

"Lift my head." His voice rasped strangely.

Her fingers slid beneath his ear, and his sight rose.

He could see the rocks now. The orbs were inside them. They'd returned to their fractures and pockets. Once again, they were dim and lifeless.

Wiley looked at his arm, struggling to focus. It felt raw, stripped of its skin. But there was no damage to see. No wound, no blood.

What's happening to me? he thought. Why had they done this to him?

"Help me up," he rasped.

Nadja turned and spoke to someone else. There were others in the room— He tried to separate their voices, but couldn't. Then hands were on him, shifting his back and shoulders.

The room's ceiling came into view. His orbs, the orbs of

flesh and blood freed in the night, were floating up there, drifting above him.

Nadja turned. She gestured and spoke to someone beside her, acting oblivious. Couldn't she see them? Did she understand how his body had been ravaged?

A face swam beneath Nadja's, eyes fixed on him. An ancient face, a troubled face. Startled, drained— His sister. Kandace. He could separate her voice from the others now. Sid had come, Sid his half brother. Bending over him with a puzzled expression. And the man with sandy curls, the reckless lonely one. Wiley could see the doctor now, in his white coat, talking to a nurse.

Were they all blind to what had happened?

The doctor approached. Greven, Wiley remembered.

"Good morning." The doctor's smile had a hint of wonder. Greven was surprised he'd survived the night.

"I'm still here," Wiley said.

"We're glad about that."

But Sid and Kandace— He could see them clearly now, and they didn't look glad. They looked wary, fretful about when death would strike him again.

Nadja was stretching beside him, holding him, cheek to his shoulder, her hand on his chest. "It's a gift," she said.

She wasn't thinking about the orbs. She was thankful he was alive.

The minutes might have been hours or days. People appeared and vanished. Wiley was alone with his questions. He wearied himself with them, without getting answers. He spoke to the scarlet orbs drifting above him. He queried his body, in whole and in parts. He pleaded with the pearls resorbed by the rocks.

When Nadja brought him lunch, she helped him sit up. He spoke to Roan and Kandace, and when Greven appeared, he told a bad joke. It had been a good joke once, but he'd forgotten the ending.

The doctor laughed and turned to Roan. "How's the chest doing?"

"Better," Roan said.

After lunch, Wiley napped and dreamt about the orbs, a dream unlike any before. The orbs were lifeless gems. He had imagined they dissolved Craag. He had imagined they would do the same for him. But he was dying without magic or mystery. The pearly orbs were frozen in the rocks, and when he'd breathed his last, his body lay lifeless on the hospice bed, still and intact.

Wiley woke from the dream, chilled, feeling empty, defeated.

He parted his lids and rolled over, wondering what he would see.

The cloud of orbed flesh was hovering beneath the ceiling. He felt a rush of relief. And then the dread returned. Would the pearlies attack him again that night?

As evening approached, Nadja crawled into bed, and he huddled against her, drawing comfort from her presence.

Slowly the window darkened. Sleep found him. Or something like sleep.

As moonlight entered the room, the pearly orbs emerged from the rocks. They coasted over the bed and settled slowly, covering his body, finding their places. His breath huffed, and his limbs shook.

Jittering, the orbs worked themselves in, burrowing and buzzing. His insides rose, gleaming red orbs freed in spouts and billows. He tried to cry out. Was anyone there?

The pearls drilled through his hands and tilled his legs. He could feel them moving the bars of his chest, digging between, waking fresh agonies. They delved in his belly, his backside, his groin. He didn't dare move.

The sound of their excavations mounted. They were humming inside him, sliding between the tightly-packed organs, foaming through clefts, bubbling in cavities. His jaw gaped, his center heaved, twisting and clenching, trying to expel them.

His open chest was a pomegranate with its rind flexed and its beads bristling. The air above him was thick with red orbs. Below, his dwindling body lay helpless, buried in pearls. All that remained was a map of pain.

From Wiley's ruined chest, a moan rose.

"I'm here, here," Nadja said.

He was trying to see—

"You're with us," Roan said, stooping over him.

"It's the orbs," Wiley gasped. "Get them away from me."

Nadja raised a glass of water to his lips, but he pushed it aside.

"The orbs," he insisted. "They're taking me apart."

Roan faced the cave of piled rocks, then he turned to Nadja. She looked frozen, with the glass in her hand, lips parted, eyes blank.

Wiley felt Roan's strong arms sliding beneath him, lifting him up.

"Open the door," Roan said.

"Get them away from me," Wiley groaned.

Nadja hurried to the door and swung it open. Then Wiley felt himself moving, the orbs sliding off. They turned as one—fish eyes, watching him through the steam.

Into the hall and along it. Roan was carrying him.

"They'll follow me," Wiley rasped.

Through the lobby windows, the sky was paling.

Wiley felt himself trundled up the stair. Strong arms, breath huffing, sandy curls— The sage eye met his, its golden spokes flashing.

"You're alright," Roan said.

"Is it morning?"

Wiley felt the pain easing. He grew calmer as they ascended. On the second-floor landing, the first rays of dawn shone through the window.

Was it over? Would the orbs go back to their rocks?

Doors were passing. Roan halted before one, then they were through it. The strong arms shifted, and Wiley felt himself settling onto a bed. His hands were shaking, but he was no longer gasping.

"They're gone," Roan told him.

He went to a window and opened the drapes. Wiley could see the sun rising.

Nadja hurried through the doorway. She approached the bed. Kandace and Sid followed her.

"I'll get the doc," Roan said.

Nadja embraced him. Wiley clung to her. She was shaking too. She held him close, without speaking.

A few moments later, Greven arrived. The doctor gave him an injection, checked his heart rate, put a clip on his finger and a cuff around his biceps.

As Wiley watched, the doctor's movements slowed. So did Nadja's and Roan's. A haze gathered around them. Nadja grabbed Roan's arm. As the haze grew thicker, Wiley heard their voices in the hall.

"He's afraid of them now," Nadja said.

"He's afraid of dying," Roan answered.

"He had all his hopes pinned on them," Nadja said.

Then the voices faded to nothing.

"Would you like some breakfast?"

An icon of beauty congealed in the air above Wiley.

"I can't eat," he rasped. "My stomach is gone."

Nadja, he thought. Then his sister, Kandace, moved beside her, and their two faces blurred.

Wiley planted an elbow and lifted his shoulder. Roan was standing a few feet away, watching him.

"Where am I?"

"It's a spare staff room," Roan said. "I've been sleeping here."

"We've moved your things," Nadja said. "This will be better for you."

The rocks, Wiley thought. His dream of bliss, his last hope—

The door opened, and Greven entered. Sid was behind him, but he paused in the doorway, as if afraid to come in.

"You're safe." Nadja clasped Wiley's hand.

Greven was preparing an injection.

"There's blood on his lips," Nadja said.

"He bit his tongue," Greven answered. "Where's the pain?"

"They were digging inside me," Wiley rasped.

Kandace closed her eyes. Sid stepped beside her.

She was right, Wiley thought. The orbs were making his death worse. Much worse.

"It needs some furniture," Nadja said.

Greven nodded. "We'll move in a sofabed and some chairs."

Wiley felt the pinch. He gazed at his arm, seeing Greven's needle going in. The flesh hung loosely, but it looked intact.

"Don't leave me," Wiley begged Nadja. He found Roan, making the same appeal with his eyes, feeling his isolation acutely.

"I'll be here," she said softly.

For the rest of that day, bodies came and went, translucent shadows shifting around him. Their voices reached him from a distance, flowing into each other. Unidentifiable, except for Nadja. She remained close, holding his hand, murmuring, stroking his temple.

Wiley closed his eyes, and when he opened them, Roan was there.

The room was dim. Roan was in a chair beside him.

"Nadja's getting something to eat," he said.

Wiley felt clear. He sat up slowly, looking around. Night was falling. The moon was rising. Its pallid light filtered through the gauzy curtains, covering Roan with webs.

"Where are the orbs?" he rasped.

Roan leaned forward. "Don't worry."

"They're still downstairs," Wiley said. "Aren't they."

"They're downstairs," Roan nodded.

"No one understands," Wiley said glumly.

"You'll be safe here."

"No one," Wiley repeated.

"Maybe I do, a little."

Roan pulled his chair closer.

"I understand you feel beaten," Roan said. "This is all too much."

His face grew larger and larger. It filled Wiley's view.

"I understand you're afraid," Roan said.

Wiley looked into the sage eyes. Strength, he could see. Isolation, intensity— And kinship. Wiley could feel it, finally. The younger man was opening up.

"Tell me what happened in the Cove," Wiley said.

"There were times I felt confused," Roan said. "Out of my head. Frightened."

Wiley grabbed his arm. "Tell me."

Roan squinted. Arguing with himself, Wiley thought. He was smothering the truth in disbelief and denial.

"You saw them come alive," Wiley said.

"No."

"You have to tell me."

"I was spooked," Roan said. "The frogs, the rain, the sleepless nights—"

"And the orbs."

Roan nodded. "And the orbs. There were times my mind skipped the track."

Wiley remembered the noises he'd heard, the ringing in pools, the endless chirping— Was it the frogs and the rain, or the sound of the orbs as they rose from the trench?

"The men," Roan said. "They were superstitious. When Imran left—" The eye with the golden spokes flashed.

"Henri," Wiley said.

Roan sighed. "I had to do some things, to keep the project going." There was a note of shame in his voice.

"What things? What happened?"

Roan looked away.

"I saw you with them," Wiley said, more sure than ever that Roan had secrets to share. "In the trench. Chanting. Naked. The fish eyes, the orbs, were rising around you."

Roan shook his head, alarmed, bewildered.

"You knew what they were," Wiley said. "Why didn't you tell me?"

"Please. Calm down."

"The wound in your chest. The orbs did that."

"The orbs had nothing to do with—"

"They're destroying me," Wiley begged. "I have to know."

"My cut was infected, I had a fever—"

Roan was trying not to frighten him, Wiley thought. And Roan didn't want to frighten himself. Like my night in the warehouse, Wiley thought. Roan had seen crazy things in the Cove, things that belonged to the realm of dreams.

But what did it matter? It was too late now.

The sky is dark, he thought, and the moon is up. They were coming.

"Too late," Wiley murmured. He sank onto his shoulder and closed his eyes.

His senses grew cloudy, his weary mind flagged.

He heard a door close. Then he was settling into the unguarded pause that heralds sleep.

They're stirring, he thought. All at once, Wiley knew.

In the room he'd abandoned on the first floor, they were rising from the cave of rocks. They drifted past an empty bed, ascending slowly, floating toward the ceiling. Wiley could see them touch the plaster and bubble through it. Then they were weaving through walls and doorways, making their way to the room where he lay.

The first orbs swam into the air before him, their concentered rings pulsing. Hordes followed, gleaming and frosting, bumpering together, deforming like jellies as they gathered eagerly around him. They touched his eroded body in a hundred places.

Then the excavations resumed.

The familiar jitter mounted, lower, graver now, echoing in the shell of riddled flesh. Bloody orbs rose in clouds from a dozen places. So much of him had already been hollowed out. They were inside his chest, dissolving his lungs. They were inside his bowels, dissolving his entrails. They were inside his heart, dissolving its chambers, consuming what remained of his spine and his marrow.

And his mind, the crown of his nature—

That too, they were turning to ruins. Wiley was helpless. His mind had holes, and through the holes, his memories were leaking. What would be left?

Nothing, he thought, *nothing*—

Then the orbs fell silent. The jittering ended. The night was still.

Time had stopped. He was in a place he'd never been, listening. A rushing sound invaded his senses.

A fountain lit the darkness before him, frothing and silver-white. Beside it stood the figure of a man, tall and broad-shouldered, with a narrow head. He gleamed like red jelly.

Wiley took a step toward him. The man recoiled with fear, and the movement made his body stretch. It narrowed in the middle. Then, as Wiley watched, the man's body collapsed. His shoulders sank, his stomach melted into his hips. Wiley stepped closer, his walking stick tapping the pavers. Did he think he could help the man? He was a few feet from him now.

The man's body glistened with multitudes of tiny red bubbles. It was losing its shape. One of the legs was melting around the other. One arm was crimped, elbow in the groin, fist raised in a quivering gnarl. Wiley extended his hand to help the man up, clasping the red appendage.

The man's limb felt cold and loose, and as Wiley tightened his grip, it mashed between his fingers. Wiley stared at the smear in his palm. The red beads glistered like fish eggs and smelled like sulfur. The man's wrist stump shook, beaded clear through.

The Caviar Man swung his arm and his twisted back lifted. Could he hear Wiley's thoughts? Was he angered by them? A rattling emerged from the Caviar throat, like pebbles in a clawing undertow. With reflexive revulsion, Wiley raised his stick and brought it around, slicing through the Caviar middle, parting the Man in two, beads flying in gobs. Blood, slime, the stench of decomposition—

Wiley attacked the Caviar head. It rolled as he struck it, red lips leering, brow dividing like a bad pudding. He struck it again, and the face fell apart, loose orbs scarlet and lifeless by Wiley's foot.

As his last stroke came around, Wiley realized the face was his own. The Caviar Man was him.

5

He was waking from a deep sleep. A sleep that might have been weeks or months.

The sensations he felt as his awareness returned were different than anything he'd known as a man. He wasn't parting his lids, taking a breath, lifting his head. Images reached him from every direction. He had no breath, and no head to lift.

I am many, Wiley thought. Dots, spheres, thousands, millions—all separate and disconnected. Was he still Wiley? Yes, but—

This Wiley was larger, and the borders of his thought and feeling reached so much farther. The old Wiley was a caged creature. The new one was expansive, dispersed—a cloud of red orbs, floating and mobile, each with a pulse of its own. The pearly orbs had transformed him.

Twinkling froth. Slippery squeaks. His orbs were glancing

against each other. Had the world changed with him? Was everything orbs and slurry? How much time had passed?

He imagined a face resolving through dimness. There was care in its eyes, and the warmth of connection. *Nadja*, he thought.

He recalled the hospice. He saw it now, far below, like a doll's house or a loaf of bread. That world hadn't changed.

His mind cleared, and the earth drew closer.

He was in a room, hovering over a bed. Wiley wasn't on it. Wiley was here, above—a cloud of orbs, dissolved and floating. Red and glittering, the beads billowed and skeined in every direction. All that remained of his earthly self was a shadowy figure, motionless, silent, its head on the pillow.

Was this death?

A wonderful thing.

The end of thought was hard to imagine. The inner voice, the true self—where could it go? The puzzle was solved. It survived the body.

Joy— He could feel it in his orbs. They rubbed and squealed against each other, rippling like jelly. *Craag*— The bliss he'd seen in his friend's face—

It was finally his.

The orbs and their gift. Wiley, the man—that fearful fool—

What had he known of freedom or the vastness of life?

Nadja stood by the bed, the morning sun on her front. She was holding the hand of the man on the bed. They had once called him "Wiley," but he was only a shadow now, a withered body beneath the sheets. Nadja looked like she was trying to smile.

I'm alright, Wiley thought. And the thought resonated through the orbs around him—a kind of speech without words, infusing the scarlet cloud. On the bed below, the shadow man shifted and its jaw moved. "I'm alright," it rasped, doing its feeble best to mimic the real Wiley.

Can you see me? Wiley asked.

Again the shadow man's jaw moved.

"Of course," Nadja said.

She was speaking to the withered creature on the bed. A muscle twitched in the shadow man's face. Its brow creased. There was still some life in it.

You're looking at my remains, Wiley said. *That poor fellow is finished. Turn your head up, Nadja. I'm in the air above you.*

The words were too much for the shadow man. Its lips struggled. All that emerged was "I'm in the air above," and a strangled croak.

Nadja regarded the shadow man, then she lifted her chin and gazed at the ceiling.

Do you see me? Wiley asked. The shadow man echoed his words.

Nadja was silent. Then she nodded slowly.

Wiley wondered, *Could she?* Nadja would bend herself around any reality, no matter how strange, for love. And there was love in her eyes now, not recognition. The orbs—and the new Wiley—were invisible to her.

Roan was at her elbow. Kandace and Sid stood with a nurse on the other side of the bed.

They've done it, Wiley told Roan.

"What have they done?" Roan asked the withered body.

I've dissolved. I'm like them.

Roan lowered his ear, trying to parse the shadow man's words.

I'm orbs, floating—

"You're pleased?" Roan asked.

Kandace stepped closer to the shadow man, her eyes wide. She looked at Sid.

Pleased, Wiley answered. He was calm, at peace, disconnected from human things and human thoughts.

It was this I wanted. His words seemed to fill the air and settle on those below. *I'm with them,* he told Roan. *Thanks to you.*

"You're not in pain?" Nadja asked, speaking to the withered body again.

No, Wiley replied. *This is what we hoped for.*

He saw the relief in her eyes.

A knock sounded, and the door opened. Dr. Greven was making his rounds.

"How is he this morning?" the doctor asked, approaching the bed.

Kandace eyed him gravely. Sid shook his head.

"His blood pressure is higher," the nurse reported. "He's stable. Better."

"He's found what he was seeking," Nadja said softly.

The day was a dream, and Wiley drifted through it. His orbs smelled things that no human could. They moved in a realm perfumed with plum, almond and violet, while those in the room below endured urine, ammonia and rank bed-sheets. The orbs' gasps and whistles breezed and lulled him, but harsher sounds travelled through him as well. The scuffle of shoes, a cough or a sneeze, a rumbling belly or the clatter of a tray.

He told Nadja the noises bothered him, and she asked them all, including the day nurses, to remove their shoes and speak in a whisper.

The conversations with him were brief. A question, a comment, a long pause between. The shadow man was always a step behind, struggling to keep up, so Wiley clipped his words and spoke slowly to make it easier on them all. No one, not even Nadja, said what they were thinking. Every word was edited before it was spoken. Despite their assurances that they saw him floating above them, Wiley knew they didn't. Their eyes were directed at the wasted husk on the bed, and they saw only its affliction.

As the day advanced, Nadja and Kandace seemed to grow closer. In the late afternoon, they were sitting together, speaking softly.

The words filtered through his orbs, with an altered mood. The voices sounded frank and forlorn.

"I'm not handling this well," Kandace said. "Any of it." She gazed at the shadow man. "His voice is different. His eyes, that faraway look— The way his fingers move—" She turned to Nadja. "Is this my brother? Has he already left?"

Nadja took her hand.

"He's not a stranger to you," Kandace said.

"No. He's the same to me. I can feel his spirit. We're still connected."

She was speaking to him, Wiley thought. He could feel the connection.

"I misjudged you," Kandace said. "You're the perfect woman for Wiley. You understand his obsessions in a way I never could."

"He attaches himself," Nadja said, "and he doesn't let go. He was like that with Assam silk. And the white crane. And me."

"Will you tell me how you fell in love? I'd like to know."

Nadja raised her head. "May I?"

Yes, Wiley thought. And the shadow man mumbled an assent.

"I'm the oldest child," Nadja said. "My father had ambitions for me. He did business with Wiley and thought highly of him. He persuaded him to give me a job."

Nadja halted, self-conscious. Wiley felt her discomfort.

"Go on. Please."

"I had dreams, fantasies. Mother said they would get me in trouble. Wiley's mind never stopped, and he was fiercely curious. He had adventure in his heart, and he'd been all over the world. I'd never met anyone like him. I fell first, but he came along quickly."

The orbs around Wiley pulsed and misted. The morning they met, the first time he looked into those deep brown eyes—

"We were on the rim of Gandikota Gorge," Nadja said.

Memories, memories— Was it a story Nadja was telling, or was he telling it himself? The shadow man rolled onto his side.

"The sun was going down," she remembered. "'I want to marry you,' he said."

"'But I'm a creature of impulse,'" the shadow man rasped.

Nadja whimpered. The sound tugged at Wiley.

A mournful silence. Then Nadja was speaking again.

"'So am I,' I said. He faced the Gorge. 'It's the edge of the world, and we're going to jump.' Wiley grabbed my waist. 'Ready?' And we jumped."

Wiley felt himself drifting with the orbs. When words sounded again, they came from a distance.

"It's a shame," Kandace said. "I wish he could stay—for you."

"He's at the edge of another gorge now," Nadja said. "With the orbs. I can't go with him."

"I lost him a long time ago," Kandace sighed. "He asked me what I expected, coming here. I think I imagined the old wounds could be healed."

"Maybe they can be."

"I was hoping he'd say he was sorry."

"He can hear you," Nadja said.

"No. It's not right. He's the one who's dying."

The room grew dim. Nadja's voice faded to nothing.

"We were close when we were children," Kandace said. "When he was a baby, I cared for him. I was only seven, but— He was my baby too."

The next morning, Wiley felt buoyant and refreshed. His sister was curled in the chair by the bed. She yawned and stood.

"May I hold your hand?" she murmured.

Kandace, he thought. Oh Kandace. Did she want him to pretend? His hands were gone. Now Sid was beside her. He'd brought her something to eat. A pastry with a red center. Cherries perhaps. Sid nodded to the shadow man, doing his best to be cheerful.

Dr. Greven was behind them. "How do you feel this morning?" he asked the thing on the bed.

Never better, Wiley thought.

The doctor didn't look up. He was content—his patient wasn't in pain.

Being dissolved, Wiley thought, had given him a new perspective. He'd never seen people so clearly, in such detail. His fish eyes focused and felt, weighed and shifted, naturally, without guidance or direction.

Nadja appeared now, with Roan behind her.

There was sympathy in Roan's eyes, something like kinship—a desire for contact Wiley had never felt from the man. Roan seemed to sense something the others could not. He was blind to the orbs. He doesn't have the vision I had that night in the warehouse, Wiley thought. But he felt the new Wiley as no one else did.

Has death frightened Roan? Has my estrangement touched him?

My life, Wiley thought, was full of people. Now I'm as alone as he is.

Wiley gazed at Nadja.

Look up, he thought. And the shadow man croaked, "Look up."

Nadja lifted her face and smiled. The morning light sparkled on her teeth and her eyes. She was beautiful, and confident as ever. Too young to accept death gracefully. Too grounded to believe the orbs were real. She had done everything in her power to deny her youth, to muzzle her fears, to erase her doubts. With Nadja, there had never been secrets. She had been his constant when life stretched before him, and now, despite everything, she was still his mate.

Would she care for a dissolved man any less than a whole one? No. Nadja was thinking about the future. Their future together.

But even as these thoughts bloomed, he knew they were woven with self-deception. Amid all his tender sentiments, there was something troubling. This woman he felt so close to— She was feeling his absence, not his presence.

His love for Nadja was free of morbid fears. He had found a blissful state, and part of that bliss was knowing it would last forever. He was still lucid. He was still with her, even in his disunion and elevation. To dissolve was to change, and changes occur in every life.

But that wasn't what Nadja thought. Like everyone else, she thought he was leaving.

Will you come closer, Wiley asked. The shadow man motioned.

Nadja moved closer. Her steps were soundless. She was wearing her Indian slippers with the curled-up toes. She was a creature of magic, a dream of Scheherazade. With her in it, the room was a welcome place for one who'd dissolved. He drifted above her, detached and free. Below, her voice rose out of a silver lake.

"I'm here," she assured him.

Nadja's deep brown eyes were as soft as her voice.

Minutes passed, hours perhaps.

Nadja was gone. Sid was seated beside the bed with a black book in his lap.

Sid raised his head and moved his lips.

"Fix your eyes not on what is seen, but on what is unseen," he said.

Sid couldn't see the orbs or feel what Wiley felt. But his heart was with him.

"What is unseen is eternal," Sid said.

It was a wonderful thing they shared, Wiley thought. All of them, even the hospice staff. No one had anything else to do, they all wanted to be close to him and each other. But it was sad as well. They spoke and acted as if his time had passed, without considering some new possibility.

I'm in the orbs' care, Wiley explained. *Eternity is their home.*

"Eternity," the man on the bed groaned.

Sid halted his reading.

"Eternity," the withered creature repeated.

"Are you sure you don't want dinner?" Nadja stood in the doorway, holding a tray.

That body, Wiley told her, *is like a pair of worn out shorts, fallen around my ankles. I'll be glad to be rid of it.*

Nadja glanced at Sid. "Changing his clothes. Tending his wound. Putting lotion on his feet. I remember when he could stand on them."

Please, Wiley thought, *stop caring about that. I'm dissolved.*

"Dissolved," the dying man murmured.

"Dissolved," Nadja echoed, approaching the bed. "Just

orbs, floating and glad to be free." She was like a child reciting the rules of a fantasy she knew to be false. "I want to believe. If you were well, you could convince me."

"I'm going to do puja," Nadja said. "Is that alright?"

Wiley's orbs drifted above her, loose and detached.

She and Kandace stood by the dresser. A platter was on it.

Kandace drew things out of a sack and passed them to her, watching as Nadja arranged them.

Why this, why now? he wondered.

Nadja's hair was damp. Wiley remembered: her grand-mother did puja when her father died.

A cup of rice, a jar of spice, a bowl of butter, and a pair of white flowers. When the platter was full, Nadja lit a candle and held a stick of incense over the flame.

Kandace watched.

A ritual for comfort, Wiley thought. Nadja was going to mourn for him.

The perfumed smoke coiled up. Pungent, woody and soapy— It mingled with his orbs and their scents, waking memories of the mists over Lake Alaotra, and the fumes that wandered the Ganges' banks. In that land of mystery that had given him Nadja, bodies came and went like wraiths, emerging suddenly, vanishing in the darkness.

"Is there anything I can do?" Kandace whispered.

"You're supposed to sing," Nadja said, "but I don't know the mantras. You could hum something, if you like."

Kandace nodded.

Nadja bowed her head and moved her hand around the platter, touching the rice, the butter, the flowers.

Kandace began to hum. The melody seemed to rise from inside her, not from her thoughts, but from a deeper place, where the wishes of the heart are stored. It welled from her chest up into her mouth, where it slid between her tongue and palate. A moment of recognition, of surprise, then she closed her eyes and let the tune have its way.

Wiley remembered the song. A lullaby. Mom had sung it to him when he was a child. And so had Kandace.

It was poignant. They were feeling his loss.

But he was still with them. Why were they acting as if he was gone?

The price of bliss on earth, Wiley thought. He'd never felt so detached, so distant. So alone.

Was it later that day, or the following?

Sid led a man and woman into the room. The man was elfish, in a gray suit. The woman wore a lumpy blue sweater and a long dress, and held a basket in her hand. They faced the withered man on the bed, assuming that was Wiley.

Sid introduced them. They were from a mission of mercy, down the highway.

"The soul has a life of its own," the elfish man started.

"The body dies," the woman said. "The soul lives on."

The soul, Wiley thought.

115

"Do you believe in heaven?"

"Yes," the withered body replied. I'm in heaven now, Wiley thought.

The woman felt for the cross on her sternum.

"I've dissolved," the dying man rasped.

"Shall we pray together?" Sid said.

The man and woman knelt, and so did Nadja and Kandace. Roan watched from the doorway. Then, as the prayer began, he stepped forward and lowered himself.

The theme was the bond between people. The prayer was for love, love for a friend, love for an enemy, love for a stranger. Then Sid's voice rose, and his prayer was that all men and women might "love one another as brothers and sisters." His eyes were closed, but his voice was firm and resonant.

The timid man was revealing himself. Wiley was touched.

In the middle of Sid's prayer, Kandace reached for Nadja's hand.

A heavy rain fell at twilight. The sky remained clear in the east, and when the moon appeared, it lit the flowing cliff. Cascades poured from its top, streams gushed from its cracks, sheets varnished its walls.

The wasting body lay unconscious beneath the sheets. Roan was seated in a chair by the bed. Wiley floated above, watching.

The room was humid, strangely damp. There were beads of sweat on Roan's brow, and the floor looked slick. As Wiley watched, the windows fogged and began to drip.

What's happening? he wondered.

Roan shifted his feet. The floor beneath was rippling.

Pearly orbs were rising through it and emerging from the wall behind. Wiley saw throngs of them gliding through plank and plaster, flowing into the room.

Why are you here? he thought.

The pearly orbs approached the bed. Strings of them rose like jotted fingers, encircling the motionless body. Longer they grew, longer and taller, reaching toward Wiley's scarlet orbs. A forest of fingers— Then the fingers merged, and the orbs were a pearly cordon surrounding his floating corpus. The soft spheres crowded against him, pulsing and squealing, mingling with his own.

He was fully dissolved. What more could they do?

A wing of his scarlet self— Wiley felt the pearly orbs pressing against it, jittering, coaxing. They were herding a part of him, bearing it toward the exterior wall. All at once, he could smell the night and the canyon. He could feel its damp. He shivered at its chill.

Part of him was leaving the hospice.

Wiley's mind froze, his spirit cried out.

The withered body on the bed was bucking and twisting. Roan came to his feet.

Pearly orbs corralled more of the scarlet. Another island

of Wiley was pulled. Craag, Wiley thought. Another piece of himself was being borne away.

Roan stood below, his hands on the body that writhed on the bed.

No, Wiley begged the orbs. Please— I'm happy the way things are.

The orbs were listening—they felt his dread. But they were still pulling.

Anguish, regret— Heartbreak spread through him, and with it, consciousness returned to the dying man. The withered body shook in Roan's arms.

"They're taking me," it said.

Roan's face was chalky.

"The truth," the dying man gasped.

Roan was shaking. His mask of self-assurance had come loose.

"Tell me," the dying man said.

"The natives— They thought the orbs had some kind of power. There was a sacrifice. Henri cut my chest."

"Dyeen man," the shadow rasped.

"I pretended," Roan said. "To get them to work. I lied, I pretended. That's all."

The Maiden, the beach, Wiley thought. The fish eyes had a mission. But it was too late now— The pearly orbs were overwhelming him. He felt their frosty haloes and smelled their violet essence. Islands of him were departing, and as they did, they took his awareness with them. Roan's voice was dwindling.

Henri knew, Wiley thought, seeing the aged face, feeling his reverence.

Nadja's cry reached him. She had entered the room. She threw herself on the bed, clasping the shadow man with retching sobs. "Don't let them," the dying man wheezed. And then that, too, faded.

The pearly orbs were crowded thickly around him. They were escorting him into darkness, through the damp and the cold.

The canyon was ghostly. The flotilla passed the Old Y and mounted a rocky saddle. Below, the thread of a highway trailed to nothing.

The hospice was behind him. There was only moonlight, the drowned air and a world of shadow gliding beneath. Forward, a vanguard of pearly orbs led the way.

It's over, Wiley thought.

The orbs were listening. They could feel his sorrow. But they weren't slowing or changing course.

I'm not coming back, he thought.

On either side, the pearly masses flattened and staggered, eaving like the crowns of windswept trees. Some moved silently, intent on the course. Some bubbled and chirped against each other. Some felt his distress and pulsed with emotion. All bore him incurably farther into the night.

Urban hives, asleep but glittering. Foggy cropland, drenched fields. Cities shrinking to towns and villages. Roadways knotted and tangled, fraying to nothing. Rumpled mountains, cloudy forests, crusted plains— The earth that mankind inhabited passed beneath him. The movement of the shepherding orbs was fluid, calm and deliberate. But it was happening quickly.

The last outposts of man, the lights winked out. Petering barrens, the waste of the pole— Until all that remained of the world was a freezing mesa, shelved with ice.

Where am I? What am I?

His orbs shivered, infused with dread.

Like an infant cast from the womb, he struggled to distinguish himself from the home he had left. What belonged to his vanished harbor? What belonged to him? Had he ever been patient or doctor, seller or buyer, lover or son—

No.

He was froth, orbs, dreaming potential. Without gender, species or earthly mark. He was droplets of mind, drifting in space.

This is really the end, Wiley thought.

6

*N*adja woke suddenly, unsure where she was.

Moon glow. The room in the hospice. The rain had stopped.

How long had it been? Roan had left, and so had the night nurse.

Wiley was beside her, motionless. She felt his hand and his face. Both were icy.

He isn't gone, she thought. Not yet.

She pressed herself closer and put her arm around him. Was he shivering, or was it her?

"Wiley," she whispered.

He didn't respond.

She cleared the damp hair from his brow. "Wiley."

Was her voice reaching him?

"Not yet." She put her hands on his chest, entreating—

Wiley, the orbs and the puja gods or any others who might be listening. "Don't leave me."

The door opened. The light snapped on, and the nurse stepped forward.

"He looks chilled," the nurse said, buzzing for Greven. "I'm going to wrap him in blankets. Will you help me?"

Nadja shook her head, refusing to remove her hands.

"We can make him more comfortable," the nurse said, trying to shift her arms.

"He's still here," Nadja said.

"Yes, he is. Wiley's breathing." The nurse put Nadja's fingers on his neck. "You can feel his pulse."

Greven arrived two minutes later. He checked Wiley's blood pressure.

"It's sinking," he said. He turned to the nurse. "Let's alert the others."

Nadja, lying beside him, watched him closely. As Roan entered the room, Wiley rolled onto his back and his breathing stopped.

"Doctor—"

Wiley's chest convulsed, and he devoured the air.

"This isn't uncommon," the doctor told her. "We may see some tremors."

Wiley's mouth was open. His eyes were sealed. Again his breathing stopped.

Silence. Another deep suck. Nadja put her fingers over his heart.

Roan stepped forward quietly. He looked at Greven.

The doctor said nothing. His jaw was set, braced for what was to come.

Ten minutes later, Sid and Kandace arrived.

Kandace approached the bed, reached for Wiley's hand and clasped it.

His eyes remained closed.

"If you have things to say," Greven urged her, "I would say them now."

Nadja rose from the bed. She sank into a chair, with her head in her hands and began to sob.

Sid looked on, grave and silent.

Kandace spoke haltingly, as a grieving adult at first. Then her voice grew simpler and happier, talking about things from an earlier life. "Your sister looked out for you. Do you remember? I'd stand up for your crazy stories. You were always in trouble. I adored you for that. I understood you better, then. My little Wiley—"

When she was done, Sid took her place. "Brother—"

There was no reply.

"Does he know I'm here?" Sid asked.

"He knows," Greven said.

Sid regarded the dying man, then he closed his eyes and bowed his head, speaking silently to Wiley perhaps, or to God, or them both. Then he stepped back beside Kandace.

Greven took another blood pressure reading. "Still declining." He turned. "Roan?"

Roan was surprised at being invited to join the grief. He hadn't known Wiley long, but it was true—he felt close to the man. The orbs had made him a partner in Wiley's departure. He approached the bed.

Where are you now? Roan wondered. In the dream you tried so hard to make real? Roan hoped he was.

Wiley's mouth was slack. His wind chucked in his throat.

"The goal is in sight," Roan said. "You'll be there soon." He put his hand on Wiley's shoulder.

As Roan backed away, Sid smiled at him. Kandace watched them, mystified, her eyes as innocent as a child's.

Greven nodded and faced Nadja.

"No," she objected.

Roan turned, and so did Sid and Kandace.

"He's still here," she said stiffly, rising and stepping beside the bed.

She stroked Wiley's temple. Then she drew the covers back and slid in beside him. "I'm not ready," she said to him.

The nurse glanced at Greven. The doctor stood motionless, watching Nadja. Sid looked at Kandace. The older woman closed her eyes, as if to confess her unfitness. The silence stretched out.

Finally Greven gestured, and Kandace and Roan followed him into the hall. Sid remained in the room with the nurse and Nadja.

"This may require some patience," the doctor said.

"I've made arrangements with the funeral home," Kandace said. She looked at Roan. "I was wrong about the orbs.

They helped him." She sighed. "Maybe you knew him better than any of us."

"He wanted his rocks," Roan said.

"That's not what I meant."

"The closer he comes to death," Roan said, "the more I understand him."

The hall was silent.

Kandace was squinting at him, guessing, suspecting. The doctor wore a sympathetic expression.

I've said something revealing, Roan thought.

He nodded to them and turned, stepping down the hall, muddled, feeling the rift he so often felt. *The closer he comes to death, the more I understand him.*

Roan reached the stairs and started down. As the lobby came into view, it struck him. Only a man facing death was as alone as he was. It was Wiley's isolation, and his courage in facing it, that he understood.

As he approached his sleeping quarters, he saw a crowd spilling out of the room next door. Inside, Mrs. Linaje sat in her wheelchair, overdressed as always, with her face made up. On her bed was a birthday cake with candles burning. Family and friends, mostly women, chattered around her like a flock of siskins.

A teenage girl with a topknot turned toward him, reaching into a paper bag. She handed him a stick with a rainbow streamer.

Roan shook his head. "I'm not related."

The girl blushed and smiled, revealing her green braces.

The pearly flotilla escorting Wiley had stretched and narrowed, turning into a river. It glided smoothly at first, then it rushed, gaining speed. The frothing orbs had hurried him between midnight banks. Then abruptly, the river widened. The current's momentum tumbled him over and over, and the rushing faded.

No— I'm not ready. Wiley, Wiley—

A familiar voice had made his orbs ring. Its crying emotion still echoed in the gaps between. His journey had halted.

The red orbs floated in a quiet inlet. The lighting was dim. The pearly orbs had been dashed in every direction.

I can't leave, he thought.

Pain held him. Pain and need. He could feel it around him, urgent, oppressive. No matter where the orbs wished to carry him—

He couldn't go.

The Inlet fed a sea, and the sea was before him, its waves rolling, furling and folding. The Dark Sea of the Cosmos.

As he watched, the pearly orbs gathered themselves, forming clusters again.

What were they doing? Conferring, rehearsing—

How long would they wait, thwarted, suspended?

How long would he remain there, stranded and marking time?

"I understand what you're feeling," Greven said.

He stood by the window on the second floor landing, speaking to Nadja. Kandace and Sid watched on one side of her. Roan was on the other. Two days had passed since the parting words they'd given Wiley.

"I've seen this before," the doctor said. "It's not a good thing." He spoke gently, but firmly. "He's still sensing the emotions around him. If you're unwilling to let him go, he's going to struggle to stay alive."

Nadja looked at her hands, as if something had fallen from them.

"He wants to leave," Sid offered.

"You don't need him," Nadja said.

Roan faced her. "He's reconciled. The orbs—"

"Damn them," she barked, raising her fists before her. "We thought they would help us. We thought—" She cried out. "Don't I matter?" Her eyes darted, searching for someone who fathomed what was happening. "I'm losing everything. It's all dissolving."

Kandace approached the bed. "Are you awake?" she whispered.

127

Nadja was lying beside Wiley.

"You must be hungry," Kandace said. "Let's have some breakfast. Roan will come get us if there's any change."

"I'm not leaving," Nadja said softly.

"I thought we might make lunch today for the nurses. To show our appreciation. They've done so much—"

"Can't you understand?"

Kandace looked at Sid. He was seated in a chair by the window, with the black book in his lap.

"I'm feeling sorrow." He spoke to the room. "For Nadja, for Wiley. For all of us. Matthew says, 'Blessed are those who mourn.'" He looked at Nadja.

Wiley's head turned on the pillow.

Nadja shifted her face before his eyes, listening for sounds.

Kandace stepped closer. "Please," she begged, "come away."

Nadja raised her shoulder, as if any contact with Wiley belonged to her. "We have time," she murmured. She slid her hand inside his shirt, over his heart. "Sing the lullaby," she said without turning.

Kandace stood silent. Then she looked at Roan. "I'm useless."

"Leave me alone with her," Roan said, glancing at Sid.

Sid raised himself, and he and his sister departed.

Roan stepped toward the bed.

"Nadja," he said.

She peered up at him. Wiley was stretched between them.

"He's ready to go," Roan said.

She shook her head.

"You're thinking of yourself," he told her.

Nadja's features softened, accepting the accusation.

"The orbs are his destiny," Roan said. "He's counting on us to serve it."

"That's a fantasy."

"You were going to believe if he needed you to."

"I did believe." Her face crumpled. "I don't want him to go." She began to sob.

"What if it wasn't a fantasy," Roan said.

"Listen to you." There was a note of scorn in her voice.

"Wiley would want us to believe the orbs have a power we don't understand. Wouldn't he?" Roan eyed the dying man. "He would want us to believe they have some kind of plan for him."

Above her wet cheeks, there was puzzlement in her eyes.

"Wiley thought I was hiding something," Roan said. "He thought I'd seen things in the Cove that I wouldn't disclose." He kept his eyes on Nadja. "What if I was?"

"Are you playing with me?"

"Life tethers us to this world," he said. "For some the tie is strong. You were Wiley's tether. That's why he needed the orbs."

She curdled her brow, unnerved, resisting.

"It isn't his body," Roan said. "It's his love for you that he has to dissolve."

Nadja touched the dying man's cheek. "I won't let him."

Despite her words, Roan could see her logic bending.

It had bent for Wiley, and it was bending for him. She was remembering. She'd promised Wiley.

Nadja was no longer crying. She lifted her shoulders.

"Why are you doing this?" She turned her head with a jerk.

Roan felt something break between them. Nadja was rising.

She held up her hand to silence him or fend him off, distraught, blaming him. Then she hurried from the room.

Roan stood before the dying man's bed, alone with him now.

Through a part in the drapes, the moon was full. It hovered in dawn's lilac, pearly and close to the earth, like a master orb proclaiming the time had arrived.

Roan remembered their first meeting. Wiley's blue eyes, his laugh, his tan coat and white pants— To create your own end, Roan thought. To lead yourself out of life— The man had courage. But he needed help now.

He touched Wiley's arm, then he settled on the bed beside him.

Vato Cove. The chirping frogs. The crescent of rocky beach, the crashing waves and the roaring monsoon. The sounds came back with the smell of the wrack and the swamped pools. And the images too. A rogue wave, like a giant scallop shell. The flooded trench. Henri's scraggly goatee, the rusty scissors in his chapped hand.

The old man rose like a ghost from a sealed vault, into Roan's heart and mind. Henri's faith, his gentle eyes— What were the secrets Wiley wanted to hear? When Henri snipped, the blood flowed down Roan's chest. They pledged their devotion to *les ancêtres*, and the wave swept Tsinjo's body away. All for the fish eyes, the priceless gift for a "Dyeen man."

What could he tell him?

I was sick, I had a fever, Roan thought. There were moments when I felt I was losing hold, when the Cove and the orbs didn't seem real, when I wasn't sure I would find my way back.

Roan lowered his head until his lips were a few inches from Wiley's ear, and he began to whisper.

The water was stagnant. The air was thick and heavy. Wiley felt it pressing against him on every side.

How long had he been stranded in the Inlet? Was it minutes, hours, days?

A voice reached him. A relic of thought, wandering through the stranded orbs. A familiar voice, it seemed to Wiley. Familiar, but not his own. A voice of strength and singularity.

I'm being watched, he thought. And when he turned his attention toward the Inlet's shore, he saw giant eyes suspended, peering through the trees. They were eyes he knew. Sage eyes. The iris of one had golden spokes.

They were eyes of courage, eyes of resolve. Eyes that knew desperation, and what it meant to be truly alone. They were eyes that knew the orbs' story. And as Wiley listened, the story was told.

The trench was dammed. The men worked inside it. Rain slicked their naked bodies, and the starlight made them glint. An old black man stood among the rock piles, with the sea at his back. "Fish eyes," he said. And as he spoke, a throng of orbs floated up out of the trench. They purled and pulsed in the air, rubbering against each other, chirping like frenzied frogs or a call coming over a satellite link. They watched the men in the trench swinging their hammers. And then they turned as one, peering across the endless miles, seeing his scarlet orbs, motionless in the Inlet.

"As sure as I breathe," the voice said, "the orbs are alive."

There was awe in the eyes, and Wiley felt it. The madness, the magic— It all came back. Men chanting in the rain. Silver light from a smear of moon. The Maiden of the Orbs, buoyant, jaunty. Gleaming skin and gleaming teeth, and she balanced a tub on her head with both hands free. They followed her toward the surf. And then—

The unexplainable moment. She began to rise, and he was rising with her, over the beach and the curling waves. And the orbs, the beatific orbs, the orbs of bliss—

They lifted out of her tub as if they were weightless, and were born away through the wind and the rain.

Wiley heard the native chants mingling with the voice in his head.

The waters of the Inlet were stirring. The air seemed lighter, the pressure relieved.

On all sides, the pearly orbs reappeared. Wiley saw them gliding toward him in hordes, tumbling over each other.

"Trust them," the voice whispered.

The pearly orbs drew closer, massing, gathering around him. Beyond the Inlet's calm waters, the waves of the Dark Sea rolled, furling and folding.

Some of the pearly orbs lost their pulse as he watched. The concentered rings faded. The orbs turned translucent. He could feel their jellied surfaces sliding against his own. Each one was swallowing a scarlet orb.

A frightening moment. A million translucent pearls encysted to admit him, and a million carnal orbs gave themselves up. A red orb was drawn into the center of each pearl, and the gel of the pearl engulfed it. Then the pearly orb began to pulse again, its rings compressing the orb of flesh, shrinking it to a dense red sphere at its center.

Wiley's atomized body, what remained of his broken self—blood, dust and salt—was absorbed. The pearls were marrying themselves to him, swallowing him. And along with his body, they absorbed his mind.

The man who'd become a million red orbs could barely be seen. Each of his jots was a tiny red nucleus now, inside its pulsing and pearly carrier.

A swell was lifting beneath him, a smooth hillock bearing the orbs higher and higher—

He was on the crest of a mounting wave, a blue ridge with steep sides, a giant ridge, a sharpening ridge— He was the froth at its height, churning, foaming, poised and teetering with drop-offs on either side. The gleaming edge curled over—

And the force that held him—released him.

The orbs were hurled from the Inlet into the Dark Sea.

Silence.

A boundless unknown.

But Wiley felt cared for and protected. The pearly orbs held him. They were his home. What remained of his mind felt their comfort and reassurance. And their pulse lit the darkness.

They were moving, carrying him with them.

They knew the Sea, and the Sea knew them. They were its children, its conscious expression. And like their parent, they were timeless too.

The Sea's colors thickened to chasmal purples and inky blues.

In the oblique light of dawn, the redrock cliff looked ancient, every crease deep, the stacked blocks bulging. Nothing was blooming yet in the hospice gardens, and the boughs of the orchard trees were bare.

Wiley's head rested on the pillow, pale as the linen. His cheeks were hollow, his open eyes vacant, sunk deep in their sockets. His hands lay motionless on the coverlet.

Nadja stooped over him with a washcloth. A froth of bubbles had left a dry crust on his chin.

Kandace and Sid stood with Dr. Greven on one side of the bed. Roan stood on the other.

"He's so quiet," Kandace said. She leaned toward the doctor.

He put his arm around her shoulders.

"Do you think he's still fighting?" Sid asked.

The doctor pursed his lips, as if he had an opinion but was unwilling to voice it.

Kandace looked at Nadja. "The funeral home has some questions." She sounded like someone who had misplaced something and was wondering where she might find it. She reached her hand toward Wiley's knee, then stopped and drew back.

Greven led her and Sid out of the room.

"You look calmer this morning," Roan said.

"I feel calmer." Nadja squinted, as if she was trying to understand her state. "Maybe I've given up."

"It's probably time."

Nadja nodded. "I woke up this morning wondering if he'd live through the day." She smoothed the counterpane over Wiley's chest. "I thought I could do it, but I couldn't. I couldn't give him what he wanted."

"It's not too late," Roan said.

"What do I have to give? I'm going to get some tea. You'll stay with him?"

"I'll be here," Roan said.

He watched her cross the floor on her curl-toed shoes.

Wiley was on his own now, and so was she. Without a sound, she opened the door and closed it behind her.

Roan stepped closer to the dying man.

He was hard to look at. His expression seemed frozen. His lids were open, but his eyes were glazed. Roan lowered his head, trying to peer into them.

The two men had shared something. Sympathy, under-standing— Roan had done what he could to help him. But there was no recognition now, no connection whatever.

The room was silent. Perfectly still. No movement from the dying man, no sounds of breath. "They'll care for you," Roan said.

He imagined he was hailing the dissolved man, crying out to him, wishing him well. A mass of orbs, the remains of someone the world called "Wiley," was drifting away.

Wiley lasted through that day and into the night.

The vigil disbanded at 2 a.m.

"I'm going to lie down," Roan told Nadja. "You're alright?"

"I think so."

"Sid?" Kandace turned.

He nodded, then looked at Nadja. "I would like to have known him better."

When the three had left, Nadja turned toward the bed.

She sat beside Wiley and combed his hair with her fingers, handling the strands as if they were more alive than the rest of him. His eyes were open, but she avoided them now, speaking to a Wiley who felt her close and heard her, even if he couldn't reply.

She mined her memories, as if by raising them she could secure them for the future. Memories of joy, memories of hardship, memories of humor mixed with candors and stark confessions. "I have to say these things to you," she explained, "while you're still here."

Wiley's hip shifted.

Nadja froze.

Slowly, he raised his arm. His wrist twisted. The palm turned toward her, thumb and forefinger straight, the others half-curled.

She saw a caress in the gesture. The hand, those fingers—

It was as if he'd returned to life.

"I'll always love you," she said.

A word passed through Wiley's lips, touched the air and was drowned by a sigh.

He was crossing the Dark Sea, and a vanguard of orbs was leading the way. Absolute calm—he could feel it now: the end of intention, the triumph of thought. Like the moment before sleep, when the body's forgotten and the mind's free to wander. He'd been born in the Sea, in the fluid realm of idea. They'd been distractions, distortions—all the things that had touched his mortal self.

This is my home, he thought.

And then—

A familiar presence filtered through the dark currents.

"I'll always love you," the voice of the world said.

She was tender and grieving.

She wanted so badly to keep him— But she knew this was right, and she was letting him go.

With what little remained of his corporal strength, his mind shaped a word. "Love," he said.

Wiley had come from a small place. He was part of something enormous now. A life without physical limits. The orbs that bore him had spread far beyond his earthly frame. He was growing with them, expanding as they did, dispersing through space. He could feel himself at the center and soaring on either side. He was plunging too, carried by orbs that wove through the depths.

A breeding place, a boundless womb, where ideas spring forth, where they grow and conflate— He was part of it now, and he could see the Sea's thoughts.

Ahead, through the weaving currents, a foreign body of orbs appeared. It spasmed and erected, pearls flying, flashing with welcome. His energy, his potential, the new thoughts he might engender—his arrival inspired them.

A nexus drifted over him, casting out webs of pearly froth. Intuitions, conjectures— A future unheard of. An endless wealth of reflections and speculations—

A plethora of bursts now, in every direction. Bright conceptions and glaring distortions, each with an uncertain idea winking at its core. A future, their future— The orb clouds shared fantasies about who, what, how and where.

A spontaneous swell, and veils of orbs flickered beneath him, stretching like glowing plankton, nets of allowance and mitigation—tolerance for the limits of matter, sympathy for the restrictions of flesh.

And then, in the distance, a great arc of light: a chain of thought, each new perception bursting and glowing and igniting the next, until one grand surmise spanned the Sea like a milky way, a billion orbs pulsing.

The orbs were the masters. Fate was their dream. They foretold an impossible future, and they cheered the good fortune of its fulfillment.

Wiley was finished with pain and separation.

He had joined the mind of the Dark Sea.

7

*H*ad eons passed, or had the journey occurred in the gap between sighs?

However long it took, the migration was ending.

Through a million watchful eyes, the far shore came into view.

There had been orbs to excavate Wiley and orbs to lead him across the Dark Sea. And there were orbs to guide him to his resting place.

The concentered pearls, each with a vestige of him at its core, began to descend.

Drops, he thought. Each a little more dense than the element in which they swam. They drifted down and landed gently, settling against each other. All around them, the lip of a circular canyon rose, as if a woman had balanced a great tub on her head and the orbs were descending into it.

An hour before dawn. At the edge of the curtains, a slice of the moon still shone. Nadja was seated in the chair beside the bed.

Her head was bowed, but she wasn't asleep.

She sat upright. What was it?

The room had a new quiet.

She planted her feet and rose, stepping closer.

Wiley lay motionless beneath the sheets, dusted with moonlight.

His expression was peaceful.

Nadja stooped over him and touched his brow.

His head slumped, his lips parted.

His eyes were unblinking, and the glassy stare shook her. She felt for his breath, and feeling nothing, she put a forefinger on each of his lids and closed them. She looked at his face for what seemed a long time, remembering the Wiley she'd known.

Then she circled the bed, raised the sheets and stretched out beside him.

His body was warm.

She unbuttoned his shirt. Then she opened her blouse and pressed her chest against his. Was it the way you wanted? she wondered.

She kissed his cheek and closed her eyes.

It was, she thought.

She could feel his serenity.

That helped to calm her. Her heart had been like a child stamping its feet.

There was no talk left in her, and she was all cried out. So she lay there in silence.

And then, for no reason, she began to hum. She'd forgotten most of the words Kandace had sung, but as the melody ripened, a few returned. It was a foolish ditty, and maudlin too, about a kindly buffoon named Mister Moon. He visits a dreaming baby, and the song he sings is a wind that carries the child into the sky and across the heavens.

Nadja woke at dawn with Wiley in her arms.

She called Greven, then Roan and Kandace.

Roan stood on one side of the bed, Sid and Kandace sat in chairs on the other. Nadja stood at the foot, watching Greven check Wiley's vital signs as the sun rose.

Two hours later, a mortician and attendants arrived from the funeral home. They lifted Wiley onto a gurney. His skin had started to yellow. They secured his body and drew a sheet over him, then they wheeled the gurney out of the room.

Greven and the four mourners followed.

A long cream car was backed up to the hospice entrance. The attendants paused at the threshold, collapsed the gurney and carried Wiley over it, all without a word being spoken.

Kandace began to weep—loudly, sharply—a sound of protest, but hopeless, knowing there could be no relief. Nadja descended the stairs, following the attendants as they loaded Wiley into the car, as if she was unwilling to entrust him to strangers. Roan came up beside her and grasped her hand. Greven stood by the cab of the car.

The mortician and attendants climbed in, Greven squeezed the driver's arm, and the car crunched over the gravel, moving slowly toward the highway.

"Nadja." Kandace shook her head. Her tears were piteous now, messy and unrestrained. She wept like a child while Sid held her.

"To love your brother," he murmured, "is to live in the light."

"I'll miss him," the doctor said.

Nadja was staring at the spot on the gravel where the car had parked.

Two men stooped beside what remained of the orb rocks in the room downstairs. Together they lifted a large one, wrapped it in cloth padding, and lowered it into a crate. One of the men was unshaven. He was chewing something. The other was thick and muscular, with a grimy shirt. He set the lid on the crate, and the other hammered the nails in.

The thick man sealed a smaller box, hefted it and stepped

through the open doorway. The unshaven one slid a hand truck under the crate and wheeled after him.

Roan was kneeling on the floor by two rocks, taping bubble wrap around one. Sun streamed through the window at his rear, lighting the orbs of the other. They were no less vivid than when they'd been removed from the trench. Each was a world of color, concentered rings and interior light.

Nadja appeared in the doorway, wearing flats. The curl-toed slippers were gone.

As she stepped toward him, he finished wrapping the rock and placed it in the open crate beside him, the last to be filled.

"I kept this with me, at Wiley's request." Nadja raised the finger-shaped fragment with the five orbs. "It's yours now."

"I don't need them all," Roan said, standing.

Nadja eyed the fragment, then shook her head. "I have no use for it." She stepped closer and slid the fragment into his shirt pocket.

"Where are you taking them?" she asked.

"To a storage locker in Tucson."

"You're going to sell them."

"That's the plan," Roan said.

She folded her arms around her middle. "It's like giving away his clothing."

"Have you ever been to a gem show?"

Nadja's locks, dark and uncombed, dangled beside her ear. "Why would I do that?" she muttered.

"You could see the orbs go into the world."

She shook her head. "My treasure's already gone."

Roan reached his hand out.

She clasped it.

"I'll feel his absence every hour of every day," she said.

"He left his mark on me. I won't forget. I cared about him."

She let go of his hand. "I'm thankful for all you've done."

"He got what he wanted," Roan said.

"You don't know that. Do you?"

Roan didn't reply. Part of him wondered. Part of him wanted to ignore his doubts.

"What did you say to him," Nadja asked, "when the two of you were alone?"

Roan met her gaze. "I remembered your words. 'The season of facts is behind us.' I stepped into his dream. To help him let go."

Nadja closed her eyes. The idea that, in his final hours, Wiley was lost in another reality distressed her now.

"Belief is a powerful thing," Roan said. "The natives in the Cove— They believed, because of Henri." His words were tentative, feeling their way. "He was a man of conviction, like Wiley. He believed his ancestors had a plan. Without Henri's belief, the orbs would still be under the beach. No day laborers would have done what they did."

"What does that matter?" Nadja spoke softly, to herself. "He's gone. The beliefs mean nothing. The orbs are worthless to me."

"They meant a lot to Wiley," Roan said.

Nadja raised her brows. "Hold onto a few. You never know."

The cynical tone pierced him. Roan turned away.

"When you leave here," he said, "where will you go?"

"Back to New Delhi. For me, the world is small again."

When the last crate had been wheeled to the truck, Roan left the room. Mrs. Linaje's door was open, and as he passed, he could see people sitting quietly within, reading while she slept. The teenage girl with the green braces appeared, stepping through the doorframe with a lunch tray in her hands. Roan met her gaze and smiled. She blushed and laughed.

At the hospice entry, he knelt and pulled out the door stop. Then he crossed the threshold and swung the heavy door on its hinges, shutting it behind him. The truck was backed up against the steps. Its bed was piled with boxes and crates, and the workers he'd hired were seated among them.

Roan raised his head, feeling a biting gust, slitting his lids against the harsh light. He was back in his world, the unpeopled home of wind and sky. As he descended the steps, the stone building behind him seemed like a poor deceit. It gave the impression of permanence, but those inside knew better.

He started the truck and pulled out of the parking lot. It crunched down the gravel drive, and as it approached the highway, it picked up speed, raising a cloud of dust. One of the men in the rear opened a can of beer and handed it to the other. And then the men, the truck and its crated cargo disappeared.

At the rear of the hospice, the first green shoots had emerged from the flower beds. In a few short months, the lantana would bloom and the beds would be splashed with color. Fruit would hang from the orchard trees. They were leafless now, but there were warblers in the branches, eager for spring, newly arrived from the south. People would sit on the porch in the late afternoon and watch the light change in the canyon.

At the bottom of the slope, the stream glittered like an aisle runner woven with jewels. Where it touched the bank, the flow gurgled and pleated; and from the damp soil, the first columbines had sprung. A swallow *churred*, hovering around a slot in the redrock cliff. The castellations were striped with rills, and ferns hung from the seeps.

A large tree rose at the head of the canyon, a tree with two giant boughs. One pointed at the cliff, the other arched toward the valley. A woman in a black sari stood at the base of the tree, with her hands on the trunk. Above her, the twin crowns were turning green. The old cottonwood's buds had burst, and the heart-shaped leaves were showing.

ROAN
IN THE
COVE

*T*here was no escaping the chirps. Behind the rain and beneath it, surrounding his brain on every side, the air rang with chirps—a million self-important claims, echoing in tiny throats. The satellite phone wasn't bleeping, but the chirps made it hard to tell.

Roan opened his eyes and raised himself, standing on his knees in the dark tent. It was hot and humid, and the unceasing drops tapped on the canvas. He pulled on his rubber boots and his rain suit, drew back the flap and crawled outside.

Past midnight, and heaven for frogs. From every pool and rill, every hill and hollow, and from the drenched forest surrounding the Cove, the chirping cacophony rose. Roan was exhausted and nettled. He needed more sleep. There was only so much you could lose.

The crescent of rocky beach lay two hundred feet below. The sand dunes came and went with the tides. Seven headlamps were shifting over the rocks, and a dozen nightlights glowed. Beyond the surf, two boats bobbed at anchor. Waves slapped the hull of a racing launch, and a beacon on the cruiser pulsed. The sea glittered with phosphorescent foam, as if alive to their presence.

He donned his headlamp and switched it on, stepping toward the huddle of tents on a hillock fifty feet away. Provisions and tools were heaped behind, under a shuffle of tarps. Clucks sounded from a pen of chickens. As he approached, Roan could hear a man snoring. The perfume of a night-blooming flower reached him. He turned on the trail he'd cut days before and started down to the beach.

He had entered the country secretly, on a prop plane from Cape Town. In Jangaville, there were soldiers in the streets, but no one had stopped or questioned him. The people were mostly black, but there were Asian and Indian faces, and white ones too. He'd hired a foreman to rustle up a team while he combed the street markets, buying food and equipment. In the harbor he met a fisherman who spoke English. Quickly, quietly he'd rented the boats. They'd loaded the launch and cruiser before dawn, and by first light, they were out of the port, headed north.

Reaching the Cove, with all it would take to mine the vein, was easier than he'd expected. The problems began once they arrived. The Cove was physically unremarkable—a dark crescent between two points. Landing should have been easy, but a sequence of accidents befell them. As they were ferrying things ashore, using the launch and a small inflatable, a sneaker wave overturned the launch. They lost a good portion of their food. The inflatable was punctured and they had to repair it. It was above the surf now, secured to a rock. The campsite they chose slid from beneath them the first night, and they spent the next day digging their equipment out of the mud.

Wiley was proving to be a difficult client. He wanted to talk, constantly. Roan had bargained him down to one call a day, but the only way to charge the sat phone's batteries was to motor to the cruiser and fire up its engine. "I'll call when I have something to report," Roan told him.

Problems with Imran, the foreman, surfaced soon after their arrival. In Jangaville, the man had seemed a good pick. He spoke French; he claimed he could round up a team quickly, and he'd lived up to his claim. But in the Cove, giving orders, Imran was arrogant and officious. The men bristled at his insults.

Roan had fanned the team out, following the shoreline, digging sounding pits in the gritty soil. They worked when the tide was low, at midday and in the middle of the night. They'd been at it for nearly a week, shoveling sand and earth from the pits, abandoning them when the tides swept in; and there was still no sign of the orbs.

As he reached the beach, Roan saw one of the men waving a night-light. The man set the light down and came forward, crossing the rocks, balancing on bare feet. He had something under his arm.

It was Tsinjo, with the lopsided face, a broken jaw that had healed badly. He did the work of two, but he craved attention and talked too much. Now he was shouting. Men rose from the pits, and their headlamps converged.

Roan strode toward them.

Imran reached Tsinjo. The talkative man held up a thin rock, the size of a dinner plate. Roan couldn't tell what Imran was saying, but he seemed to be asking questions. Tsinjo ignored him. He spoke to the others in the native tongue, as if what he had to share would raise their regard. Then he put the rock in another's hands, and they passed it around, pointing and flaring their eyes.

Imran saw Roan approaching. He grabbed the rock, made a show of examining it, then turned and presented it.

"*Pour toi*," Imran said with a toothy smile.

In the light of his headlamp, the plate-shaped rock looked badly weathered. Between lumps and pitting, Roan saw orbs. They had lost their luster, and the concentered shells were broken—but the gems were unmistakable.

"*Montre-moi*," he told Imran. "Where did he find this?"

Imran faced Tsinjo and loosed his pretensions on him, waving his arms, speaking harshly. In his blue beret, camouflage pants and running shoes, the foreman looked comical.

Tsinjo ignored him, motioned to Roan and turned. Roan, with the others, followed Tsinjo to a pit where the rock had come from.

Roan knelt to examine it. When he rose, he faced Imran.

"*Ce n'est rien*. It's nothing," Roan shook his head. Tsinjo's rock had broken loose of the vein years or centuries before. "*Retourne au travail.*"

Roan could see the men reading his reaction. Their faces fell.

"*Je suis heureux*," he said to Imran. "I'm pleased with our progress. Tell them that."

Imran threw the plate-shaped fragment to the ground, shouted at the men as if they were children and waved them back to the sounding pits.

The rain beat harder. Roan pulled the hood over his head. As the men returned to the diggings, he could see the fatigue in their movements. He checked his watch. They had eighty minutes. Then the tide would come in, drown their pits and drive them back up the beach.

The double shift drained the men, and the rains kept them drenched, but they settled into a rhythm. Every night, Roan's sleep debt grew. He had snored through quakes in Peru. In Java, kingdoms of night grubs crawled across his chest. What was it about the Cove? Was he losing his grip? The frogs waited for him to drop off, and as soon as his mind fogged, the rain began to drum and the chirping resumed.

At twilight, on the tenth day of digging, a man named

Kalepa struck a ledge of rock four feet beneath the surface. Kalepa—*homme chat* as Imran called him—was tall and slender, and his movements had a feline grace. He spoke little, but the others seemed to respect him.

Through Imran, Roan ordered Kalepa to clear the soil around the ledge and assigned Tsinjo to help him. Two hours later, Roan was down in the hole with a hammer and a bucket of water. His first swing revealed the glassy matrix. The second freed a fragment, and when he turned it beneath the light on his forehead, he saw a cluster of orbs.

"*Lumières,*" he barked. "More light. A *pointe* and a sledge."

Imran translated the order and men leaped across the rocks, collecting the night-lights and ringing the hole with them. Imran lowered the spike and a long-handled sledge.

Kalepa watched Roan with a hunter's eyes. Like the rest, he'd refused rain gear. His threadbare shirt and pants covered his wet body like a second skin.

Roan showed Kalepa where to set the spike and ordered Tsinjo out of the hole. Then he raised the sledge with both arms and brought it down. The rock split, and a chunk came loose. Roan nodded to Kalepa and climbed out of the pit.

Kalepa raised the chunk to him.

As the beam of his headlamp touched its surface, Roan's breath caught in his throat. Pearly orbs were swarming between his thumbs. The men gathered close, fingers pointing, speaking with hushed and wondering voices.

A distant chattering sounded behind Roan.

He turned.

A dark cloak was rising from the forest. It rucked and unfolded, filling the sky as the chattering mounted.

Imran shouted. Kalepa clambered out of the pit.

The noisy cloak was drawing over the beach. Grunts, gurgling—

Creatures were flying over them, large as foxes, with tapered heads and leathery wings. Bats, larger than any Roan had seen or knew existed. Imran screamed and cowered. Tsinjo was jabbering. Kalepa looked from the bats to Roan. An older man dropped to his knees, face turned up, his ball cap clasped in his hand. He looked stunned, overcome with emotion.

"What is this?" Roan said.

"*Les ancêtres,*" Imran cried.

"The bats?"

Imran watched the dark cloud spreading over them with terror in his eyes. The others seemed confused, fearful, uncertain. Kalepa stood shaking his head. Tsinjo was edging away from the beach, his eyes on Imran.

"You're spooking them—"

"*Les ancêtres!*" Imran turned to flee.

Roan grabbed him. "Calm down. Listen to me—"

"*Ne me touchez pas,*" Imran hissed.

"*Fou.* You fool."

Imran flung his hands over his head. "*Fou?*" He sneered, jabbing his chest with his fingers, screaming epithets in his native tongue, eyes wide. He raised his face, following the bats.

Then Imran tore himself loose and took off running.

At dawn the next morning, Roan stood in the forest with the satellite terminal at his feet and the video screen in his hand. The air was warm and the trees were dripping. The frogs had asserted their rights all night, and they were still asserting, hopping on the ground, through puddles, over the trunks and branches of the trees.

He drew a deep breath, trying to settle himself.

The giant bats had circled the beach and returned to the forest. When they were gone, Imran and the others huddled at the south end of the Cove. They returned to their tents at the end of the day. Roan didn't approach them. For men who lived with military rule and the plague, their distress was hard to understand.

When he woke that morning and crawled out of his tent, the men were gathered at the shoreline. They were watching the inflatable motoring away. Imran had taken it.

The terminal bleeped, locking on the sat signal. Then the dialer began ticking.

Important progress, Roan thought. He needed to focus on that and let the obstacles ride.

The screen flashed, and Nadja's face appeared.

"I'll wake him," she said.

A moment later, Wiley swung into view. "News?"

"We found it."

Wiley stared at him.

Roan raised the hunk of rock he'd split off and held it before the camera's eye.

"Good god," Wiley sighed.

Roan saw the weary eyes close. Wiley's relief was profound.

"This came from the water's edge. The vein is headed inland. All we have to do is follow it. We'll give it everything we can at low tide. Once we're higher on the beach, we may be able to run a full shift in daylight."

"How much have you mined?" Wiley asked.

"This is it, right now. There will be more the next time I call. I can't speak for the quality of the material. I'll know better once we've removed a few hundred pounds."

"How large do you think the vein is?"

"No idea. We just struck it."

"Can you show me? I'd like to see it."

"Most of the vein's still buried," Roan explained. "We have to trench around it."

Wiley's unyielding desire for the gems hidden in the Cove was a mystery to Roan. The man had only a few months to live.

"I wish I was there."

"No you don't," Roan said half to himself.

Nadja spoke softly. "You look tired."

"I could use some sleep. The rain won't let up. And the frogs— It's like being sick and delirious."

"You're not on the beach," Wiley said.

"I'm on the hill above, in the forest."

"How's your team?"

Roan was stone-faced. Wiley sensed trouble.

"Everything's fine."

"Tell me the truth," Wiley pressed him.

Roan peered at the camera eye. "Imran's gone."

"Where did he go?"

"Back to Jangaville, I suppose. He took the inflatable."

"Why?" Wiley asked.

Why was the question, Roan thought. Why giant bats? Why did the natives call them ancestors? Why was this happening with the vein in reach?

"Nonsense. Crazy fears," he said. "I'll sort it out."

"I thought Imran was the only one who spoke French. How will you talk to them?"

"I said, I'll sort it out."

Wiley was silent.

"I'll call you when I know more," Roan said.

As he disconnected, a breeze grazed his neck, raising the hair on his nape. A sudden suspicion—something was near, listening, watching. He turned.

A troop of lemurs, black and rust-colored, were descending from the trees. Their blue eyes were on him, curious, unafraid. They gathered beside a trickle, cupping their hands, carrying water to their lips. He put his back to them and started down the slope.

When the Cove came into view, the men were standing together on the beach.

They saw him coming and retreated to the far side of the

pit, with the vein at its bottom. As Roan drew closer, he could see the fear and distrust in their faces.

Eyes hard, straight-lipped, he stepped around the pit, into their midst.

"Who here speaks English?"

Silence. Tsinjo cocked his lopsided head.

"Or French. *Qui parle français?* Anyone?"

More silence. Kalepa, the tall *homme chat*, glowered at him.

Roan scanned the faces. He needed someone to pull the group together. "Chief," he said. He put his hands to his chest and made a show of swelling it.

Kalepa took a step forward. He grasped Roan's arm and led him toward the oldest of the group, the man who had fallen to his knees when the bats flew over. He was small, with nappy gray hair, a ball cap and a scraggly goatee. His nose was too big for his face.

"Henri," the old man introduced himself, extending his hand.

Roan shook it. "Talk to me."

Henri made a helpless expression.

A reliable worker, Roan thought. The old man's movements were measured, as if every exertion had its cost; but he kept a steady pace. What did he know of the bats and their appearance?

"*Les ancêtres,*" Henri said in a reverent voice, as if he could read Roan's mind. He looked up at the sky, following the path the giant winged creatures had taken.

Roan nodded. *"Les ancêtres."* Then he cocked his head and wrinkled his brow, expressing his puzzlement.

Henri looked into the pit and pointed at the glassy surface where Roan's hammer blow had uncovered the orbs.

Roan gazed up at the sky and then down at the glassy fracture. Henri nodded.

"Maso ny trondro," Henri said. He pointed at his eye and then back at the glassy fracture. "Maso ny trondro." He made a searching face and turned his head from side to side with his eyes bugged, as if trying to peer through some medium denser than air.

Roan shook his head, stumped.

"Nahoana?" Henri squinted at Roan, acting out his puzzlement. He looked into the pit, and then he tracked the beach, gazing at the others. "Nahoana, nahoana?"

"Why?" Roan guessed. "Is that the question? Why are we doing this?"

"Why," Henri repeated the word.

"For a dying man," Roan said. *"Homme malade.* Dying."

Henri regarded him. "Dyeen."

Roan nodded. He let his jaw drop, put his hand to his heart and slumped.

When he looked up, Roan saw a sudden depth and clarity in the old man's eyes, and the recess of some still deeper question.

Roan picked up a shovel. He handed it to Tsinjo and eyed the pit. Then he turned to the others and motioned, hoping they would grab their spades and join in. "The vein," he said.

Henri stepped up to Tsinjo and took the shovel from him. He turned to Roan, shook his head and set the shovel down. Then he motioned to the men, and they followed him up the slope, back to their encampment.

Roan watched them go, weighing his options. Finally he drew a deep breath, picked up the shovel and descended into the pit. While the tide was out, he worked alone, clearing what soil he could from around the vein.

Six hours later, Roan followed the trail back to his tent. The rains had returned shortly after he began to shovel, but he took the beating. He was drenched now, and covered with mud. He halted before his tent and stripped off his shirt and pants.

When he pulled back the flap, he saw Henri seated inside.

"Good," the old man smiled.

"Make yourself at home," Roan said, crawling in.

Henri scooted to the side and passed a dry cloth to Roan so he could dry himself. He seemed at pains to show his respect, but his manner was poised and confident.

"Ready to go back to work?" Roan wondered aloud.

Henri put his hand in his coat pocket. He drew his fist out, and when he opened it, Roan saw a half-dozen fish eyes. Roan lived on the chickens they'd brought. The men trolled from the shore and ate what they caught.

"Maso ny trondro," Henri said.

"Fish eyes," Roan pointed.

"Fish eyes," Henri repeated.

The eyes were like the orbs, with their concentered shells. Again, Roan saw depth in the old man's gaze. What was he trying to tell him?

Henri put the fish eyes back in his pocket, then he touched Roan's chest.

"Dyeen man," Henri said. He bugged his eyes and turned his head from side to side, as if searching, like he had by the pit that morning. "Fish eyes," Henri nodded. "*Les ancêtres.*" His eyes brimmed with awe and veneration.

The orbs were allied with the ancestors. *Les ancêtres* could see like fish. Or the orbs were like eyes. They brought sight. Magic sight. Roan's mind was a tangle of speculations.

"Fish eyes," Roan said. "Good."

"Good," Henri intoned. "Dyeen man."

"For the dying man," Roan said.

"Dyeen man," Henri nodded gravely, and he swept his hand between them, following the gesture with a look of compassion, as if applying his idea to a mass of humanity.

Could fish eyes help the dying? What did the ancestors have to do with it?

"They're okay with us taking them," Roan said to himself, half hoping. He crawled to the tent opening, grabbed a shovel and drew it inside. "Work," he said, holding the shovel before Henri.

Henri nodded. "Work. Joro."

"We're going to help all those dying men," Roan said.

Henri gave him a beatific smile. "Dyeen man."

Roan peered into Henri's eyes and, as he did, the eyes seemed to lose their bed. Deeper they went, deeper and deeper, as deep as the man himself. And deeper than that. It was as if Roan could see through Henri's faith into some hidden realm. The abyss of death, the ancestors' cave, the unbounded darkness of superstition—

Henri slapped his knee and crawled out of the tent.

When Roan descended to the beach the following morning, the men were seated around the pit. They rose as he approached.

Henri stepped forward. His smile was reverent, humble. He removed his ball cap, looked at the group and made a show of putting it on Roan's head. He opened his arms and embraced Roan. "Work," he said. "Joro."

Roan patted Henri on the back and scanned the group. Tsinjo smiled. Another man eyed the vein down in the hole. Henri motioned to Kalepa, and the tall man began to clap. One by one, the others joined in. Roan didn't understand, and then he did. They were applauding themselves. Henri faced him. Roan raised his hands and clapped along.

Was it as simple as that? he wondered. The earth around the vein had to be trenched. He retrieved a pair of shovels.

Henri was frowning, shaking his head.

Roan halted. What was wrong?

"Joro," Henri said. He made fists and held them against his chest, exhaling with a stricken expression.

"Joro," Kalepa nodded.

Henri shifted his gaze around the group. "Joro."

The others agreed. "Joro, Joro."

"What is Joro?" Roan frowned.

Henri knelt and picked up a broken shell from the beach. As he rose, he tested the shell's edge with his thumb. Then he straightened, held his hand out, and slit the top of it. "Joro," he said, looking at Roan.

"Blood?"

Henri dabbed his finger in the droplets. "Blood," he repeated. He faced the pit and pointed his bloody finger at the vein. "Blood."

"Joro," Kalepa urged the men. And they concurred, "Joro, Joro."

Henri swept the air with his hand, including them all, and ended by settling on Roan's shoulder. The old man's eyes glittered.

"No," Roan said. "Not on your life."

Henri considered him carefully. His expression was thoughtful, not surprised, not angry. He raised his brows, reached up and took the ball cap off Roan's head. Then he sighed and turned, and the men followed him back to their shelter.

Joro was performed at sundown. Roan insisted the natives go first. There was mistrust in Tsinjo's eyes. Kalepa was scornful. They seemed offended by his ignorance. Henri persuaded the men to make allowances.

Kalepa started things. He removed his shirt, and then he and Henri climbed into the pit. Kalepa stood facing the vein. The others, Roan included, knelt at the pit's rim. Henri looked into the sky, as if it was still black with bats, and uttered what sounded like pleadings. Was he asking the ancestors for pardon, seeking forgiveness for something Kalepa was going to do? Or assuring them the man had good intentions?

Henri drew something from his pant pocket. As he raised his hand, Roan saw a pair of rusted scissors. Henri grasped Kalepa's biceps. He pinched a vessel on the arm's soft inside and snipped it. Blood spurted out.

Roan glanced at Tsinjo, kneeling beside him. His conviction seemed unshaken. Kalepa had closed his eyes. Henri was speaking in phrases now, and Kalepa repeated them. An expression of faith, a call to departed intimates, a promise to think certain thoughts or take certain actions— Roan couldn't tell what the substance was, but Kalepa's jaw spasmed and there were tears in his eyes. All the while, the

169

red rill snaked down, puddling below the exposed ledge of rock.

When Kalepa's offering had been made, he pinched his wound and clambered out of the pit, and the next man descended. Two weeks before, all they cared about was getting paid. Now, through Henri, a strange connection was being forged. Roan could feel the emotion in the old man's voice and see how deeply it affected the men. Whatever the belief was, they were going back to work.

When Tsinjo was done, he climbed out of the hole. Henri rolled up the sleeve of his shirt, exposing his wiry biceps, and snipped himself. He watched his blood dribble down, repeating the rhythmic phrases. Then he motioned to Roan.

Roan removed his shirt and descended.

Henri moved beside him, standing close. He began speaking, fast and low.

Roan raised his left arm.

Henri paused, muttered something and put his hand on Roan's chest.

"What are you—"

"Chief," Henri whispered. And he turned his eyes on him, those bottomless wells.

A morning beam lit their depths, and Roan felt again the strength of the old man's faith. Henri pinched a vein in his left pectoral. Then the scissors snipped and the blood was set free.

Dark faces lined the pit's rim, and as Henri's voice rose, Roan felt a breath of relief from them all. As his blood joined theirs below the fish-eyed rock, he repeated Henri's phrases as best he could. The letting calmed him. The blood warmed his front, and he could smell it now.

"Good," Henri purred, "good, good." And when Roan faced him, Henri's eyes spoke: *You were chosen for this.*

The ancestors were pleased.

And so were the men. He'd gained their trust.

By noon, they had made surprising progress. Roan guessed at the ledge's trajectory, and they excavated above the surf line and found it. They continued digging as the tide retreated, following the ledge and trenching around it. The natives' focus was sharp and their efforts unstinting. The ancestors' favor, it seemed, gave them strength and purpose. By late afternoon, twenty feet of the ledge was exposed.

It took four days and nights to uncover the vein. With every incoming tide, the sea did its best to undo their work, pouring sand back in. When the ledge was visible from the surf to its tapering end, the trench was a dozen feet wide and three men deep. They began to take rock, and the work got harder. They attacked the ledge with hammers and spikes, one man holding the point, the other swinging a sledge with both arms.

The natives seemed to believe Roan had accepted their faith, and he did nothing to shake their confidence. With

Henri, he wasn't as sure. There were times when he feared the old man knew his respect for *les ancêtres* was a show. Henri didn't press him, and Roan did his best to avoid raising suspicions.

The black men were strong and agile, unafraid of the clashing steel. With the shifting sands and the water foaming around them, they attacked the rock with resolve and endurance. Roan felled a dozen trees, and they erected a dam around the trench. That reduced the sea's intrusions and allowed him to lengthen the shifts.

Despite the obstacles, the excavation progressed quickly. The men were giving everything they had, and it was clear to Roan that the pittance they were to be paid had nothing to do with it. They were a congregation driven by belief, and Henri was their priest. Chatter about fish eyes, "maso ny trondro" and the "Dyeen man" was constant, and Roan did his best to dance around it, wondering what they would do if his true thoughts were known.

The natives worked in the rain and fought the tides, returning to camp, drenched and muddy. They stripped off their clothing and let the rain wash them. Roan did the same, alone, before crawling into his tent. He ate alone, at his end of the hillock. They fed on their fish and the crated stores. He slaughtered the chickens. Then, after a spell of exhausted sleep, they were on the beach, together again.

"Here's a good-looking one." Roan was speaking to the video screen, circling a small boulder with the camera's eye trained. "Orbs on every side." He set his hand on the rock, then stepped away, so Wiley could see the piles of excavated rock behind him.

"He's done it," Nadja said.

"We've started to cull them." Roan circled another rock pile, aiming the camera. "These are lower quality. Poorly silicified. In some, no orbs are visible."

"How much have you taken?"

"A ton and a half. Gem grade, maybe six hundred pounds."

"How much of the vein?"

"Twenty percent, I'd guess. How are you doing?"

"I'm confined to the building now," Wiley said.

He and Nadja explained that he had taken a fall. Wiley's face had thinned. His eyes looked desperate.

"What about you?" Wiley said.

"I'm ready to come back. The monsoon's a deluge. The waves are huge, and the dam can't handle them. The men— Their lives are at risk. We've got a good load."

Wiley didn't reply.

"I'm not sure how long I can hold this together," Roan told him. "I'm—"

"No," Wiley said. "I want it all."

Nadja's hand entered the frame. Her fingers blurred, then the screen image jittered and Wiley's face froze.

"What is that?" Wiley asked.

Roan looked down. Blood was seeping through his shirt. The Joro wound hadn't sealed. Its edges were purple now, infected. Roan switched off his screen and ended the call.

The punishing winds mounted. The torrents battered the men in the trench. Controlling the sledge was an impossible task, and holding the spike was worse. For the ones on the rim, lifting rock out, the wind sent the rain at a cruel angle. Roan was often there, taking the buckshot on his back and sides. Despite that, the weather did little to dampen the men's spirits. Kalepa swung his hammer with fresh determination. Tsinjo relayed rock to the piles faster than ever, shirt flapping in the wind, his torn pants suspended with twine. And Henri gave voice to the ancestors' pride, cheering them on.

The sea rose. The racing launch twisted on its mooring. Whitecaps pounded the cruiser's hull. Around the camp, rain blasted the tarps and flogged the stores, drenching grain sacks and cracking crates. A tent was uprooted and carried away. One night, the stormy sea overtopped the dam and flooded the trench. They dug drainage ditches and bailed with buckets. "It can't continue like this," Roan said.

Then they lost Tsinjo.

He was returning from the piles, having dumped his load. He beamed at Roan as he approached the trench. Roan saw the rogue wave rising behind him like a giant scallop shell. He motioned, but Tsinjo had no time to react. The wave struck him, swept him off his feet and into the surf.

In a moment the men were out of the trench. They saw Tsinjo surface—his head, an arm thrashing. Henri barked orders. A flurry of words and scrambling bodies, then a sprint toward the breakers. For a moment Roan thought they would all dive in, but they halted, waist-deep, and two lines were thrown. Tsinjo saw one of them, but he sank before he could reach it. And he never reappeared. The waves continued to crash, and they continued to watch, standing in the surf, seeing only curls and froth.

That night, crouched alone in his tent, the Cove seemed to Roan like an advancing madness. He felt dizzy, seasick, helpless as the deluge drowned them and the tide rolled in. The crazed frogs knew; they swarmed out of the hills, their chirping frenzied, announcing the end of the world.

Someone was shouting. When Roan lifted the tent flap, Henri crawled in. His face was dripping, his feet balled with mud.

"Go back," Henri said.

To Jangaville? Was that what he meant? I'm ready, Roan thought. They had half the vein now. Wiley could do with that.

"Fish eyes," Henri said, pointing toward the beach.

What was the old man saying?

"Go back," Henri repeated.

Roan was stunned. The old man wanted to return to the trench. And what about the others? They couldn't all be so tenacious.

Henri saw his bewilderment and reached his hand out.

Roan felt the old man touch his knee, as if to reassure him. He wondered if Henri had done the same with each of the men, solemnly, in private. Roan had always been committed to his work, to coming back with the goods, no matter the hardship. For what? Pride of achievement, courage, integrity, cash in hand. Henri was committed too. But his commitment sprang from a different source.

The next morning, streams were flowing around Roan's tent, and the storm was beating harder than ever. When he crawled out, he saw the men descending the slope, stripped to the waist. He removed his shirt and hurried for the beach.

He reached the trench as they did. Without a word, they picked up their tools and returned to work. Two men manned the buckets when bailing was needed, while the others used hammer and spike. They labored as never before, backs bent, the beams of their headlamps circling the walls. When a load was ready to be hauled to the piles, Roan climbed out, and the orbs rose into his hands. He took the blasts on the rim, hauling the smaller rocks alone, getting Kalepa's help with the larger. All the while, he kept his eye on the sea, fearful the storm might hurl him into it.

Later that day, as he returned from the rock piles, Roan heard a strange sound rising from the trench. It was rhythmic, forceful, and laden with emotion. The men were chanting.

He felt pity—they were risking their lives for so little. Their courage, their passion, their blind devotion— For what?

When they returned to camp, he asked Henri about it, using a word he'd learned.

"Manazava. What are you singing?" He repeated a phrase from the chant.

Henri responded with a long oration in his native tongue. He raised his face to the sky; he reached for the earth; then he seemed to be pulling earth and sky together. Earnest sounds sprang from his lips, and he fluttered his hands like two small birds. Roan had no idea what he was saying. Maybe the men were asking the ancestors for help; maybe they were grieving the loss of Tsinjo; maybe they sang to the fish eyes, or to Tsinjo's spirit.

Henri could see he was baffled. So the old man silenced himself and gazed at him with that bottomless look. The look of belief. Working in the raw was his idea, Roan thought. And the chanting was too. As he watched, Henri's gaze narrowed. The old man's eyes had a wish in them now.

"Eat," Henri said. He raised his hand, pretending to put food in his mouth. "Eat." He tapped Roan's chest and then touched his own. "You. Us."

The men sat in a circle in the crowded tent. Henri was beside him. At the center, Kalepa stirred barracuda heads in a boiling pot. They turned in the broth, eyes wide, nosing to the surface and diving back in, as if unaware their bodies were gone.

Roan had nothing to fear. But when he joined the circle, he did so with trepidation. He had suffered with the men to unearth the prize, but the chasm between them was wide, and they had been dealt a harrowing loss.

A wooden box with rice was passed around. Each man had a bowl in his lap. They were drinking tea out of tin cans. Roan raised his and swallowed a bitter mouthful. He felt the heat from the fire on his chest. The acrid smoke bit his nose. Henri turned to face him.

"Tsinjo," Henri said, "manana maso."

Roan shook his head. What was he saying?

Henri's brow furrowed. He gazed in the direction of the beach, considering their tribulations perhaps, the fierce rains, the angry sea, the grueling labor.

"Dyeen man," Henri said. "Tsinjo."

A ladle started around. A man scooped fish broth into his bowl.

Henri was nodding. "Tsinjo get fish eyes."

"He earned them," Roan said.

Henri put his hand on his shoulder and squeezed it.

Compassion creased the old man's face. Roan drank from his can.

Tsinjo has fish eyes, he thought. The rules of Henri's faith were a mystery, but its strength rang in Roan's heart. And he could feel it around him. That was why they chanted and labored like demons.

Few in the States would care to be the pups of giant bats. But it was easy to wish that a man's purpose might be as noble as Henri imagined, and that a belief as passionate as his might come to life inside you. Roan felt sick. Something in the tea or the fumes from the pot. Or the wound in his chest. He was sweating, feverish.

With a wave of dizziness came shame and guilt. He felt its grip closing now, the undertow pulling. He'd brought them to this dangerous place and cost a man his life. They thought they were on a mission for *les ancêtres* and the fish eyes, but he was packing the orbs back to Wiley, and from there to market.

Henri took the bowl from Roan's lap and ladled soup into it. When Roan looked down, he saw fish eyes floating in the broth. He blinked and the eyes disappeared.

Roan turned to Henri, and again he saw those bottomless wells. Eyes dark with wishes, hollow with grief, deep with knowing. Henri knew. Henri knew his accord with the men was a sham. Henri knew he was alone in the world, without faith in anything or anyone but himself.

Kalepa had a rattle he'd made from an empty can and some beach pebbles. He shook the rattle now and began to chant. The others joined in. Henri rocked, the men closed their eyes. Their voices were gravelly. Outside, the rain was crashing.

He had heard the chants day and night in the trench, but this chant was different. He could feel the sounds and emotions inside him. They reached out, they implored, they laid hold of a greater power. Now, as he listened, the phrases began to make sense. Without understanding the words, he knew what they meant.

The pot was boiling, and along with the steam, fish eyes were rising. They floated in the air before Roan. They looked at Kalepa and Henri. And now they were turning and looking at him. Their concentered rings pulsed—

They peered into his soul. There was no hiding now. They knew who he was.

Henri leaned closer, chanting louder, encouraging him. Roan moved his lips, echoing the sounds. Then his vision blurred, and he was sinking into the old man's embrace, feverish and shamed, alone and bereft. He felt Henri's arms, and darkness closed around him.

A downpour drowned the satellite terminal, so the calls to Wiley ceased. The work continued until the vein was mined out, and then strangely, the rains stopped and the sun appeared. It was as if the weather's only purpose had been to challenge them.

Kalepa swam out to the racing launch and brought it close enough to load. The men waded through the surf, carrying the rocks, and the launch shuttled them to the cruiser. By late afternoon, it had all been crated, and they were ready to leave. Roan thanked the men. They're sensing my distance, he thought. And then the men were forgotten. It was the city, its police and its soldiers, that crowded his mind.

The Jangaville docks were dark when the pilot arrived. After they'd lifted the crates into his van, Roan thanked Henri and the men again. Then he opened an envelope and began counting out cash, intending to pay them twice what he'd promised. But Henri raised his hands and shook his head.

"No," he said. "Work. Good."

Roan extended the bills toward the men, but they answered the gesture with grumbles and troubled expressions. They had discussed this, it seemed, and were of one mind.

"*Les ancêtres*," Henri said gently, as if Roan would understand.

The work was an act of piety. Roan saw the familiar look in Henri's eyes, intensely personal—the look of faith, deeper than any other. Now, so close to his departure, the sight pained Roan.

He tried again, raising the cash with a gracious nod to the men, hoping their practical instincts would prevail. No one responded. Roan stuffed the money in his coat pocket and glanced at Henri. The cost in toil and life had been high.

"Blood," Henri said. "Rain. Tsinjo. Fish eyes—"

He was reading Roan's mind. He knew Roan was returning to the world he came from, but the old man hoped he would take his faith with him. Henri was trying to smile, but there was trouble in his eyes.

"Dyeen man," Henri reminded him.

"I'm in a hurry," Roan said.

"Dyeen man. *Les ancêtres.*"

"Put in a word for me with them," Roan said.

He felt the gap between them growing. Henri's smile sagged. He raised his arms and clasped Roan's shoulders.

"I won't forget," Roan promised.

"Forget," Henri said softly, as if he knew what the word meant. Then he turned and walked away. Without a word, the men followed him.

The pilot drove slowly, past cranes and cargo on pallets. Coconut and lumber, bagged rice and coffee, cotton and cement. With his window down, Roan could hear the creaking of the sailing boats moored in the quay. They passed a military hut, surrounded by dented trucks. Soldiers were milling outside, machine guns strapped to their shoulders. Then the van was threading unpaved streets, by open-air markets with empty stalls, past lines of rickshaws and squatters' shacks, through shantytown slums with mosque minarets looming over them.

They crossed a bridge and rumbled down a long dirt road.

When they reached the hangar, the plane was gassed up and ready to go.

They loaded the plane without interruption and were airborne when the sun rose. From the co-pilot's seat, Roan could see the island's rivers, bearing iron-rich soil, bleeding scarlet into the ocean's blue.

Rich Shapero's novels dare readers with giant metaphors, magnificent obsessions and potent ideas. His casts of idealistic lovers, laboring miners, and rebellious artists all rate ideas as paramount, more important than life itself. They traverse wild landscapes and visionary realms, imagining gods who in turn imagine them. Like the seekers themselves, readers grapple with revealing truths about human potential. *Dissolve* and his previous titles—*Island Fruit Remedy, Balcony of Fog, Rin, Tongue and Dorner, Arms from the Sea, The Hope We Seek, Too Far* and *Wild Animus*—are available in hardcover and as ebooks. They also combine music, visual art, animation and video in the TooFar Media app. Shapero spins provocative stories for the eyes, ears, and imagination.